"When are you going to get over this man?"

Justin was standing, arms folded across his chest, eyes hard.

Anger rushed to Linden's head. "I'm sorry I ruined your plans for tonight, but…"

"It's not just tonight, Linden," Justin said wearily. "Every day I'm more in love with you. I want to hold you and make love to you." He paused, closing his eyes for a moment. "I've tried my best to be patient and understand your feelings." He shrugged. "I don't know what I feel anymore, except that I'm angry and frustrated." He rubbed his chin, a tired gesture.

All she had to do was put her arms around him. Justin loved her. He wanted her. But Waite loved her, too. Linden didn't doubt that, not even after what he'd done to her.

It was not easy to start a new chapter in life….

Books by Karen van der Zee

These books may be available at your local bookseller.

Don't miss any of our special offers. Write to us at the following address for information on our newest releases.

Harlequin Reader Service
P.O. Box 52040, Phoenix, AZ 85072-2040
Canadian address: P.O. Box 2800, Postal Station A,
5170 Yonge St., Willowdale, Ont. M2N 6J3

KAREN VAN DER ZEE

pelangi haven

Harlequin Books

TORONTO • NEW YORK • LONDON
AMSTERDAM • PARIS • SYDNEY • HAMBURG
STOCKHOLM • ATHENS • TOKYO • MILAN

Harlequin Presents first edition October 1985
ISBN 0-373-10830-3

Original hardcover edition published in 1985
by Mills & Boon Limited

CHAPTER ONE

PAIN stung her face and the air froze in her lungs. She gasped, lost her balance and fell heavily against the corner of the glass-topped coffee table. A sharp pain shot through her thigh and for a moment stars danced in front of her eyes.

The front door was slammed shut. Dazed, Linden lay on the floor listening to the receding steps, still too shocked to comprehend what had happened. Tears of pain gathered in her eyes.

Waite had hit her, struck her in the face. She couldn't believe it had come to that. Despite his violent tempers he'd never laid a finger on her. The right side of her face ached dully. She touched her swollen lip and tasted blood. Her teeth were fine, thank God. The swine, she thought wildly, *the rotten swine!* This was it! The *absolute* end! She'd had enough of him and his tantrums and his black moods. How *dare* he strike her!

There was blood on her skirt and she pulled it up to examine her thigh. The sharp glass corner of the table had broken the skin on her leg. Another bruise there, a whopper, probably.

It had been years since she'd last cried. Now, suddenly, there was no holding back the tears and she wept with her hands covering her face. The most serious damage was not physical. The swellings would go down and the bruises would heal, but for the rest of her life she would remember this night, see the ugly look on the face she had loved for more than two years.

Her tears finally spent, she drew in a deep, shuddering breath. Hair hung untidily in front of her face and she grimaced. *I'm the one who should have the fly-away temper,* she thought as she wiped the mass of red hair out of her face. She gathered herself up from the floor and stumbled into the bathroom, trying to ignore the pain in her thigh. It was a shock to see her face and her anger boiled again. How dare he! How *dare* he hit her!

She stared at her reflection in the mirror, seeing the grey eyes of a stranger. Never before had she seen herself like this, with that terrible look in her eyes and the swollen mouth. Never before had she felt like she felt now—degraded, violated.

She couldn't go to work looking like a battered wife. Well, she was, wasn't she? Not a wife, but battered, anyway. She couldn't stand in front of a class of twenty-two curious students who'd all be wondering what had happened to her. *Someone hit me,* she could tell them. *To be precise, it was Professor Waite Clayton, your adored, admired, lusted after, head of the Art Department.*

Nobody would believe her.

Professor Clayton would never do such a thing. He was handsome, brilliant, sexy, charming, drooled over by every female student of the college and admired by every male. A terrible loneliness washed over her. I need to talk to somebody, she thought. She sank into a chair and winced at the pain in her leg. Oh, damn, damn, damn! She picked up the 'phone and dialled.

A sleepy voice answered and she was immediately sorry for her impulsive 'phone call.

'Liz? It's me, Linden. Were you asleep? I'm sorry, I . . .'

'What's wrong?' The sleepiness had gone from Liz's voice.

'Liz . . . I . . . I . . .' Tears choked her voice.

'Linden! What's *wrong*? *Are you all right?*' Concern made Liz's voice sharp. 'Where are you? At home?'

'Yes. Oh, Liz, I . . .'

'I'm coming over. I'll be right there.'

A minute later the bell rang sharply. Liz lived in the same apartment building, two units down the hall, and she hadn't even bothered to put on her clothes. Barefoot and wearing a hooded terry cloth bathrobe, she stood in front of the door, looking rather wild with her uncombed curly black hair. Dark eyes wide with shock, she stared at Linden.

'Dear God, what happened to you?' She moved inside and closed the door, her eyes never leaving Linden's face.

'Waite hit me.' It came out dull and dry.

'In slow motion Liz sank into a chair. 'You've got to be kidding,' she whispered.

Linden looked away and said nothing.

'Why?'

Linden shrugged. 'He lost his temper.'

'He seems to be in the habit of doing that,' Liz said sarcastically.

'He never hit me before.'

Liz looked at Linden for a long, silent moment. 'Linden,' she said softly, 'what is the matter with him?'

She shook her head helplessly. 'I don't know. But I can't take anymore. I've tried, but I can't take his black moods and his bad tempers. There's something about him I can't understand and I ... I ...' She swallowed and tears crowded her eyes once again. 'I can't go on this way.'

'You love him.'

'Yes. I did, anyway. But nobody hits me. *Nobody*. Not even Waite, *especially* not Waite.' There was strength and conviction in her voice, but inside she felt a growing despair. She'd have to leave. She couldn't go on working with him, seeing him every day.

'What happened to your leg?' Liz was looking at the blood on her skirt, coming out of her chair and kneeling next to Linden.

'I fell against the coffee table when he hit me. It's not bad. I'll just have a zinger of a bruise by tomorrow.'

'Let me see.'

Linden moved up her skirt and bared her thigh and Liz whistled.

'You'd better put something on it. Why don't you get out of your clothes and have a shower? It'll make you feel better. I'll fix us something to drink, and I'll take that skirt and soak it in cold water or you'll never get that stain out.'

Later they drank the hot buttered rum that Liz had made and listened to the howling of the October wind that rattled the windows.

'I sold one of my paintings,' Linden said tonelessly. 'The red and white one.'

Liz's eyes lit up with interest. 'Did the same man buy it? The short little bald guy?'

'Yes.' He'd bought two others. He was the wealthy father of one of her students and seemed to like her work. 'Waite said the price he paid me was ridiculous. It was too high for that painting, which he considered of inferior technical quality.'

Liz stared at her. '*Waite* said that? My God, he has the tact and sensitivity of a bulldozer! What did you say to that?'

Linden grimaced. 'I said there was no accounting for tastes, and that at least somebody thought enough of my work to pay me well for it, which was more than he could claim.'

She shouldn't have said it, she knew the moment she saw his face, but she'd been so hurt and angry by his biting criticism, she'd let her emotions take over her common sense.

'Good for you!'

'Not so good for me,' Linden said dryly. 'That's when he hit me.'

Liz winced. 'He's jealous, of course.'

Linden made a frustrated gesture. 'But it doesn't make sense! He has more talent, more experience than I do. He's so much better all the way around.' She sighed. 'He hasn't painted anything for months. He's been in a horrible mood for ages. The stuff he painted a while ago was awful, not at all up to his standard. Apart from that it was morbid, depressing, which isn't his usual style. It scared me.'

'Why?'

Linden shrugged. 'It seems one more indication that something is wrong.'

They were silent. It had started to rain. Absently Linden listened to the drops pitter-pattering against the window.

'Are you going to work tomorrow?' asked Liz at last.

'No.' Linden felt her hands tighten into fists. 'I'm not going back at all.'

'You're going to quit?' Alarm sprang into Liz's eyes. 'Please, Linden, think about it first! You know how hard it is to find another job!' The previous year Liz had been out of work for months, the most ego-shattering months of her life, she'd said.

It wasn't as hasty a decision as it seemed. Linden knew the moment the words were out that the thought had been brooding for a long time. How many nights had she not lain in bed thinking, *I've got to get out, I've got to get away.*

'I know, Liz, but I just can't go back. I don't ever want to see Waite again.' Her voice caught in her throat. 'Two years is a long time. I can't go on teaching in the same building, seeing him every day.'

'What are you going to do?'

'I don't know. I'll have to think of something, won't I?'

An idea came to her later as she was getting ready for bed.

Liz had insisted on staying over, sleeping on the couch. She'd locked and chained the door, checked out the windows as if she were afraid Waite might come back and attack Linden.

Linden dropped her earrings into a small basket on her dressing table and her eyes caught the key. Her father had given her the key several years earlier and it had been in the basket ever since.

It was the key to a small wooden house on stilts on a tiny tropical island in the Indian Ocean. Pelangi Island—Rainbow Island, just off the west coast of Malaysia.

As she looked at the key, vivid memories flashed through her mind. She saw again the blue-green of the ocean, the vast blue expanse of sky, the lush greenery of the island. Tropical flowers, clove and nutmeg trees, small waterfalls, chattering monkeys, a small Chinese temple. And the islanders—an exotic mixture of Malay, Chinese and Indian people.

For six years her father had been a Professor of Urban Planning and Development at the University in Kuala Lumpur. Their vacations they'd spent on Pelangi Island, living in the small fisherman's house her father had had built by the islanders.

Her parents were both dead now. Her sister lived in New Orleans, tied down by small children and a lawyer-husband, and had no desire for travel. Linden had always wanted to go back to the island, but there'd never seemed to be time or money. She wondered what had happened to the house, whether it was still closed up and empty, or if someone had appropriated it thinking the foreign owner would never show up again.

She stared at the key in her hand.

'I'll go back to Pelangi,' she whispered.

Linden managed to leave without seeing Waite again, although he tried to contact her time and again. He had a key to her apartment so she moved out and stayed with Liz. She did not answer the door or the telephone while Liz was at work. Liz told anyone who asked that Linden had gone to her sister in New Orleans and had not left an address or a 'phone number. She packed her suitcase at a time she knew Waite had to be at the college.

The days passed in abject misery. She couldn't eat and couldn't sleep. She knew she was doing the right thing, but the pain was so great she wondered if there wasn't another way. *Give him another chance*, a little voice kept saying. But she'd given him too many chances already. *It's time I started thinking about myself*.

And so, the arrangements made, Linden flew to Malaysia.

Kuala Lumpur was as beautiful as Linden remembered, but many new buildings had sprung up in the last eight years—tall, modern structures that towered above the tropical trees and palms that grew everywhere, contrasting with the traditional mosques and Moorish buildings from the past. The mixture of multi-racial people, cultures and religions in Malaysia had always fascinated her. It lent the place an exotic atmosphere of colour and contrast, and Linden could feel the excitement rise in her as she looked around as she came in from the airport in a comfortable air-conditioned taxi.

The small Chinese hotel was still there, white and clean with the same spreading frangipani tree in front. Linden entered the foyer with its cool marble floor and its tall palms in their huge brass pots and presented herself at the desk. Fifteen minutes later a bell-boy escorted her to her room, carrying her luggage. The room was small and simply furnished. The window had a view of a courtyard where hibiscus bloomed profusely and a small fish pond gleamed darkly. There were tables and chairs in the shade, a black and white cat asleep on one.

Linden showered, and dropped on the bed, too tired
to eat. It had taken two days to get here and all she
wanted now was sleep and a rest from all the miserable
thoughts that had occupied her mind the last few
weeks.

She slept all afternoon and all through the night,
waking up at five in the morning. It was still dark. A
newspaper had been slid underneath her door and she
picked it up and crawled into bed with it. It was the
English-language *Malaysia Times*. The front page
held an article on the new budget along with the same
major international news that was probably on the
front pages of all big newspapers in the world. The
women's page was on the back and sported a recipe for
Chinese dumplings, an ad for instant noodles and an
article about the place of women in various societies
around the world. She leafed through the paper,
reading a bit here and there. Sports, arts, culture,
politics, economics, comics, including *Blondie* and
Bugs Bunny. An interview with Meryl Streep.
Advertisements for cars, office computers, watches
and refrigerators. The Jaya Supermarkets had specials
on Chivers Olde English Orange Marmalade, Johnnie
Walker Scotch and Skippy peanut butter. Welcome to
the exotic Far East, she thought, amused, and tossed
the paper aside.

She showered, brushed her teeth and fastened her
hair on top of her head. Her lip had healed. Her thigh
was still showing an impressive array of colour.
Linden tried not to look at it too often. Quickly she
pulled a blue cotton-knit dress over her head and
gathered it around her waist with a wide belt.

In the small dining room she examined the breakfast
menu. There was the famous *choke*, a bowl of rice
porridge (the menu read), complimented with fresh
farm egg, pork, fish, chicken, ginger, spring onions
and crispy *mee hoon*, or rice noodles. Undoubtedly a
healthy way to start the day, but Linden didn't think

her stomach was Chinese enough to appreciate it. She ordered coffee and toast, which was a terrible way to start the day, but the American breakfast of eggs and ham or bacon did not appeal to her either.

Not much later she was in a *teksi* on her way to the railway station, a large, impressive structure of Moorish design, to catch a train to Butterworth. From there she'd take the ferry across to the island of Penang where she'd stay the night. Tomorrow morning she'd find a boat to take her across to Pelangi Island.

The train was comfortable and she enjoyed looking at the scenery of rice paddies and vast rubber plantations that sped by the window. Everything looked green and healthy. But six hours was a long time and inevitably thoughts of Waite intruded into her mind.

'He's desperate,' Liz had said. 'And he looks terrible. As if he hasn't eaten or slept for a week. God, I could almost feel sorry for him.'

Linden didn't look too good herself. She'd lost five pounds in two weeks and spent the nights weeping with her face in the pillow. How was she ever going to get over it? And all the good times flashed before her eyes—the times of laughter and loving, the hiking trips in the mountains, weekends in Philadelphia visiting art galleries and museums. He loved her. She loved him. Oh, God she thought, I cannot live without him.

But it hadn't always been good. Black moods, depressions, outburst of violent temper, had changed the charming, laughing man into a different person. And it had become worse all the time. She'd tried everything—love, patience, tolerance. She'd tried talking to him to convince him to find help, but he had laughed at her worries and refused. He was always sorry after he'd come out of one of his awful moods. Still, he would unleash his frustration on her more frequently all the time. He was unhappy with his work, frustrated by the lack of talent in his students, by the lack of recognition of his own work. His aspirations went far beyond being the Head of the Art Department of a small college in rural Pennsylvania, but he seemed incapable of doing anything about breaking out and doing what he wanted to do.

Sitting in the train staring out at the Malaysian countryside, Linden involuntarily gritted her teeth. I can't take anymore, she thought. He refused to get help and I couldn't do anything for him. I have to think of myself now—I did all I could. *I did all I could!* But tears blinded her eyes and the ache in her chest was still there.

She was hungry when she arrived at Butterworth and while she waited for the ferry she had a bowl of Chinese noodle soup with shrimp and snowpeas which she bought from a food cart by the road. Across the water she could see Penang and the ferry slowly making its way to the shore.

Once on the ferry, it didn't take long to cross to the island. The waterfront was still as she remembered, with the Clan Piers jutting out far into the sea— boatmen and fishermen's villages built on stilts over the water. George Town, the one real town on the island, bustled with colourful life. Everywhere the shops carried vertical signs with large Chinese characters. Foodstalls by the road offered all manner of exotic foods—Malay, Chinese, Indian. Linden could feel excitement rise warm inside her. Oh, it was good to be back! She'd stay here the rest of the day, explore the markets and shops and stay at a small hotel tonight. Tomorrow morning, early, she'd take a taxi to the village of Telok Bahang and find a fisherman willing to take her across to Pelangi in his boat. If the house was uninhabitable, she'd have plenty of time to get back to the main island for the night.

She exhausted herself walking along Jalan Penang, through the Pasar Malam and the Art Gallery, where she looked with longing at the *batek* paintings and the Chinese ink drawings. Waite would like this, she thought, and the pain was back deep and sharp, and the loneliness faded the colours and the life around her.

She did not stop for a proper dinner, but bought a spring roll at a roadside foodstall and later a hot steambun with a filling of meat, practising her rusty Malay on the vendors, who were amused and impressed at the same time. She bought a couple of oranges to take back with her to the hotel, where she slept fitfully despite her fatigue, troubled by dreams of Waite, who looked thin and haggard and swore never to hit her again.

He'd made too many promises, broken them too many times. Next time he might knock her teeth out, break her arm. How could she live with the fear?

'No!' she cried out. 'No! No!' But she was in his arms and he was kissing her and she was kissing him back, wanting him, needing him.

She awoke sobbing. She sat up and pressed her fists into her eyes. 'Oh, damn,' she groaned. 'Oh, damn, damn, damn!'

The taxi drove her out of town, past the State Mosque and Kangaroo Town, the residential area for Australian Air Force people, past sweeping stretches of sandy beaches with waving palm trees and colourful fishing boats.

'What hotel do you want to go to in Batu Ferringhi?' the taxi driver asked. 'Golden Sands? Rasa Sayang? Casuarina?'

Linden shook her head. 'I'm not staying in a hotel. I want to go to the pier in Telok Bahang. I'm going to Pelangi.'

For a moment the Chinese driver took his eyes off

the road and gave her a quizzical look. 'Not many people go there. There is no hotel. It's very small.'

'I know.' One sprawling fishing village and some countryside with rice paddies, coconut groves, spice and fruit trees. That was about all. Less than a thousand people on the island. No cars, no electricity. At least there had not been eight years ago and probably wouldn't be now.

The driver let her off at the fishing wharf of Telok Bahang. Fishermen looked curiously at her suitcase. Tourists brought their cameras to photograph the colourful boats, the baskets of fish, the shaky wooden pier, the fishermen. They didn't often bring their suitcases. She walked up to the closest one and smiled.

'*Selamat paoi,*' she said, and he gave her a big grin.

'You speak Malay!' he said in English.

She held her thumb and index finger half-an-inch apart. '*Sedikit sahaja.*'

He pointed to her suitcase. 'Where are you going?'

'*Mau pergi ke pilau Pelangi.*' She pointed across the sea where the small island faintly showed on the horizon. 'You think somebody can take me there?'

He nodded. '*Bisa.*' He looked at her curiously. 'You're going to see your friend?'

'Friend? Yes, sure. I'm going to see my friend.' She didn't know what he meant, but was willing to go along just so she wouldn't spend the rest of the morning talking and explaining. But she knew what he had meant when she arrived at the island forty-five minutes later and found the white man on the wharf watching her climb out of the old blue fishing boat that had brought her there.

He was tall and lean, wearing old jeans and an open-necked *batek* shirt. He was in his early thirties, she guessed. His hair was very dark and wind blown, and his brown eyes looked at her calmly as she approached him. He seemed vaguely familiar, but she didn't know why.

Her hair was a mess and she probably smelled like fish, but then, neither of these would surprise him, she imagined.

'Good morning,' she greeted him, meeting the watchful dark eyes.

'Good morning.' He didn't smile, but looked at her intently as he extended his hand. 'Justin Parker.'

'Justin Parker,' she echoed, putting her hand in his. 'Oh, I remember now! I know you!' His hand was hard and firm and held hers only for a moment before releasing it.

He nodded slowly, frowning as if trying to remember too. 'Yes, yes . . .'

'I'm Linden Mitchell.'

He smiled, a funny crooked little smile as if he wasn't used to smiling much. 'Yes, of course, Linden.'

They'd met once before, right here on this little island. One Christmas vacation he'd been on Penang with his father and had come to Pelangi to have Christmas dinner with her family. They'd stayed the night, sleeping on mats on the floor in the living room. It had been a hilarious time. Cooking a Christmas dinner without an oven was a challenge. There was only the smallest of kerosene refrigerators (shipped over on a rickety fishing boat) without a freezer compartment. They'd eaten chicken roasted on charcoal and stove-top stuffing and canned cranberry jelly. The *kampung* chicken had been tough as uncured buffalo hide. The wine they'd brought had been off, a big disappointment for Linden. The first time her parents let her have wine, and it was bad. Some luck.

Justin's father had worked in Malaysia for three years. Justin had been at university in the States and had come to see his father only once. They'd spent a week in a luxury hotel on Penang, and two days on Pelangi. After that she'd never seen him again.

'I hadn't expected to see you here,' she said, feeling awkward.

He looked at her suitcase. 'You've come back to the house?'

She nodded. 'If it's still there.'

'It's still there.'

A thought occurred to her. 'Are you staying there?'

He shook his head. 'No. I have my own place.'

'Oh.'

He bent to pick up her suitcases. The muscles of his arms rippled under the brown skin. 'Come, I'll walk you over.'

She followed him along the beach, away from the village, past the fishing boats and the small open air restaurant where some men sat drinking beer and smoking cigarettes. The beach was strewn with old coconut husks, pieces of driftwood and shells.

Then she noticed the houses on the edge of the beach. Where once had only stood her family's house among the coconut palms, now were three others. All were typical Malay fishermen's houses, built up on poles with thatched roofs and wooden steps leading up to the front door. Potted plants stood around the yards and chickens pecked around searching for food.

'Well, look at this!' she said in amazement. 'They built a village around me.'

They walked up to her house and he put the suitcase down. 'It's not a *kampung*,' he said levelly. 'The houses are mine.'

She stared at him. 'They're *yours*? What do you mean?'

'I had them built. I own them.'

'What do you do with the other houses?'

'I rent them out.' He took her arm. 'Come, let's have something cold to drink.'

She looked at the house carefully for the first time. It looked in fine shape. Obviously someone had been taking care of it.

'Let me put the case inside first.' She took the key from her bag.

'It won't fit,' he said. 'I had the locks changed. The keys are at my house.'

'You've been taking care of the house all this time?'

He nodded. 'I couldn't just let it sit there and get into disrepair. I've tried to contact your father several times, but without success.'

'He died three years ago.'

'I'm sorry to hear that.'

She looked away, trying not to remember. 'I haven't had a chance to come over here and do something about the house. It's an expensive trip. Thank you for taking care of it. Let me know what I owe you, please.'

He waved a hand in dismissal. 'It was nothing major. Forget it.'

Well, she'd have to see about that.

They'd started walking again and he led her to his house, not far, and they went up the steps and inside the door.

The inside was cool, with a breeze coming in through the open windows. There were coconut fibre mats on the floor, simple rattan furniture with kapok cushions, several bookshelves along the wall, and a couple of kerosene lamps on a small table in the corner. A large wooden desk with a typewriter and piles of paper was positioned in front of the windows. She wondered what he was doing here on the island.

'Do you work?' she asked impulsively, gesturing at the desk.

'It keeps me from starving,' he said drily.

'What do you do? Write?'

He nodded. 'Spy novels.' There was no expression in his face.

'Oh.' Somehow she had not expected that.

'Sit down.' He waved at a chair. 'What can I get you? A Coke? Seven-Up? Beer? Juice?'

'Juice, please.'

'Mango all right?'

'Great.'

He disappeared into the kitchen and she stared after him. There was something strange about him. He was so cool and aloof. Not unfriendly or hostile, just lacking in . . . in what? Warmth, life. That was it.

It was not the way she remembered him at all. That Christmas day ten years ago came back in vivid detail. Sixteen she was, and quite impressed by Justin, this college man with his laughing mouth and warm brown eyes and his vast store of interesting stories about university life. She couldn't wait to go to college herself.

The atrocious Christmas dinner over, she'd taken him on a walk around the island, and had shown him her favourite spot near the waterfalls. It had been a half-hour hike in the hills and afterwards they'd sat down on the rocks and cooled their feet in the water.

In her girlish way she had flirted with him and the surroundings certainly had been idyllic enough for romance. He had kissed her there near the waterfalls, but he had been teasing her, and she'd known it. She was too young for him, and she'd known that too. But she'd dreamed about that kiss for weeks afterwards and weaved romantic reveries, fantasising about a passionate love between them.

All of that had no link with reality and she wasn't fooling herself with impossible hopes and expectations. It was just so nice to dream about love and to have someone to dream about.

The fantasies about Justin had died an unglorious death not so much later, when she'd fallen in love with a warm-blooded French boy at the International School in Kuala Lumpur. Bertrand stuck around longer than two days and when he kissed her he wasn't teasing.

Justin came back into the room and handed her a glass of juice. He had beer for himself and he settled down in a chair across from her.

'Are you on vacation?' he asked, his eyes surveying her face intently.

She shrugged lightly. 'I suppose you could call it that. I just quit my job.'

'What did you do?'

'I taught art at a small college in Pennsylvania.'

He looked at her shrewdly. 'A man?'

'What makes you think that?'

He shrugged. 'The look in your eyes. Your face. You don't give the impression of having had a lot of fun lately.'

Neither do you, she was tempted to say, but didn't. She only nodded. She sipped her mango juice. 'And why are you here? Hiding from the world on a miniscule island in the Indian Ocean? A woman?'

One corner of his mouth turned down in a crooked smile. 'Among other things.'

'How long have you been here?'

'Three years.'

She groaned and he gave her a funny look. 'What's that supposed to mean?'

'I hope it won't take me that long to get over it. Hell and death must be more fun than a broken heart.'

He smiled again, but this time it reached his eyes. 'Welcome to Rainbow Island,' he said.

The house looked like it always had. There was a sitting room, two small bedrooms, a kitchen, a bathroom, and a small outhouse building in the yard. The bathroom had a sink, but no taps with running water. Water was carried up in buckets from the well. Her father had rigged up some sort of primitive shower—a small tank with holes in the bottom that could be closed and opened by pulling a chain. It was still there. The kitchen had a sink, counter and cabinets, two gas rings to cook on, and the tiny kerosene refrigerator they'd brought out on a fishing boat.

The mattresses on the wooden cots had disappeared. 'They were so mouldy, I had to throw them out,'

Justin said. 'Nobody had been in the house for I don't know how long and they hadn't been aired in the sun.'

There had always been a caretaker, a village girl, while her father was still alive. Linden grimaced. 'Yuk, nothing worse than the smell of mouldy kapok. I'll buy a new one in the village.'

Linden went into the village and purchased a new kapok mattress, the cotton covering a bright pink with white roses. She bought kerosene for the refrigerator and the lamps, some candles and matches and a tank of gas for the cooking rings. It was all bundled up in a bicycle cart and transported to her house, where she found a teenaged Malay girl waiting for her. She wore a pink, shortsleeved shirt and a *batek* print sarong around her waist. She had short, shiny black hair, that curled around her ears and over her forehead. She looked at Linden shyly.

'Mr Justin sent me to help you. I will clean the house for and bring you water.'

'Wonderful! Thank you. What is your name?'

'Nazirah.'

'You may call me Linden. Let's get this stuff inside first. Then I'll give you money and you can buy a broom and a bucket and soap and whatever else you need. I'm going over to Mr Justin's house for lunch and I'll be back later.'

He had invited her to have lunch with him so she would have time to get organised. For dinner she intended to get some food from one of the foodstalls in the village. When she'd stayed here with her family they had often 'dined out' at the small open restaurants or the moveable stalls by the road, standing up or sitting at rickety tables. The food was plentiful, cheap and delicious—fried rice, skewered meat, noodle soup, spring rolls, dumplings, curry puffs, fried fish and shrimp. She was looking forward to it already.

'There's no water at my house yet and I'm filthy,'

she said to Justin when she arrived at his house. 'Do you mind if I wash in your bathroom?'

'Sure, right here. Did Nazirah come?'

'Yes, thank you very much. Is she available for employment on a somewhat longer basis, or just for today?'

'I think she'd like the job. She's the daughter of my cook and she's not working right now.'

She washed as best she could, but her appearance didn't please her as she looked in the mirror, not that it had pleased her lately at all. She shrugged, put her comb back in her bag and hung up the towel.

Lunch consisted of fried fish, rice and stir-fried vegetables, all delicious.

'Who rents the houses from you?' she asked. 'I don't remember anybody even being interested in Pelangi. No electricity, no running water and nothing to do, you know. No fancy restaurants or nightclubs or swimming pools or bars. B-o-o-o-ring.'

'People who want peace and quiet. Mostly friends of mine or friends of friends. Some others—the odd writer, honeymooners, some old-colonial types, who don't like what's happening to the East. Usually not your run-of-the-mill tourist.' He gave another one of his cheerless crooked grins. 'I've had one character Interpol was looking for.'

Linden's fork stopped midway to her mouth. 'Did you know that?'

'No. He did not offer that information, but they came looking for him here a few days after he'd left. He'd told me he was on his way to Hong Kong, but that was probably not true.'

'Do you know why they wanted him?'

He shook his head. 'They didn't tell me. I didn't care particularly.'

'What was he like? I mean, did he look dangerous?' Oh, my, she thought, I sound like a curious kid.

'He looked perfectly harmless. He made me think of

my father, actually.'

Linden grinned. 'Oh, dear, your poor father. How is he, by the way?'

'Fine. Remarried last year.' He took a drink from his water and there was a sudden, surprising spark of humour in his eyes. 'The lady breeds borzois—Russian wolfhounds.'

She liked the way his eyes lit up. 'I like people with strange hobbies. I have a friend who's into fungus—fungi. You have any hobbies?'

'Nothing strange.'

She put her fork down and frowned in concentration. 'Let me think. You collect stamps? You do needlepoint? You grow orchids?'

'You're getting close. 'I'm an amateur botanist.'

'Really? Tell me about it. You go tromping around the island and look at plants and trees and that sort of thing?'

He nodded. 'Nothing serious. What about you?'

Linden sighed. 'No real hobbies, I guess. I just paint and paint. But I like hiking in the mountains, camping out . . .' She stopped abruptly and her fingers clenched around her fork until her knuckles were white.

Waite was the one who had introduced her to the joys of the outdoor life. With Waite she'd spent long weekends wandering through the hills, fishing for dinner in mountain lakes, cooking out on open fires, swimming in clean, cold babbling brooks. All the laughter and loving and happiness they'd shared. Over, gone, dead.

Tears came into her eyes, ran down her cheeks. Damn, she thought. Oh damn, damn! She got up. 'Excuse me.' She went out on to the verandah and leaned her elbows on the railing and pressed her fists against her eyes. *Stop it!* she admonished herself fiercely. *Stop it! Stop it!*

CHAPTER TWO

THERE was the sound of steps behind her, then movement on her right. He was standing next to her.

'Sometimes,' he said slowly, 'it would be better if we could get rid of the memories along with the lover.'

The pressure on her eyeballs was creating wild kaleidoscopic designs in her brain. She removed her fists and for a moment looked blindly out over the sea, seeing nothing but shimmering darkness. Then her vision returned and she drew in a deep, breath.

'I'm sorry,' she said. 'I'm not usually so emotional.'

'Don't apologise. Shall we go in and have a cup of coffee?'

She shook her head. 'No thanks. I'd like to get back to the house and see how Nazirah is doing and then I think I'll go for a swim.' She kept her voice carefully calm.

'Be sure you don't burn,' he said. 'It's hot out there.'

'I know. Thank you very much for lunch.'

Nazirah had swept out the bedroom, made the bed and carried a bucket of water up to the bathroom. Linden dug out her swimsuit from her bag and changed. She found a towel and suntan lotion and headed for the beach. A large spreading rain tree stood at the edge of the beach and she dropped her things off in the shade of it and ran to the water. The sand burned her feet. The water glared and sparkled with the sun's reflection.

There was no one else out. It was too hot. She really would have to be careful. It was October and she hadn't been out in the hot sun for six weeks or so. The ocean was placid and the water warm. Floating on her back she squinted up at the blue sky. There were clouds coming in over the ocean. It was the rainy season and there might be a good rain later today or tonight.

She closed her eyes and thought of what Justin had said. *Sometimes it would be better if we could get rid of the memories along with the lover*. Would it not be a waste to forget all the good times? No matter how much it hurt now, she had loved Waite and he had been part of her life. It could not be amputated like a leg.

She tried to make her mind a blank. She should learn yoga or meditation. Relax the body, relax the mind. The soft movement of the water was having a soothing effect. She began to feel the tension drain out of her slowly as she drifted along on the water, using only a minimum of leg movement to stay afloat.

After a few minutes she left the water and sat in the shade under the rain tree and squeezed the water out of her hair, then shook it loose and back over her shoulders. To the right an outcrop of large boulders jutted into the sea. The rocks, worn smooth and round by the waves, looked grey and black. She had climbed those rocks as a girl, feeling the rough encrusted surfaces under her bare feet. Barnacles and shells clinging to the rock had all the colours of the rainbow when you looked closely. Once she'd tried to paint those miniscule colour clusters and had failed.

Turning away from the ocean, she examined the other little houses set back in the coconut grove. Everything looked quiet and peaceful. No one was around. Sensible people had a siesta at this time of the day. What was the saying again? *Only mad dogs and Englishmen go out in the noonday sun*. And broken-hearted American redheads, apparently.

Justin's house was closest to the beach, set apart a little from the others, with large bushes of crimson hibiscus growing on the left side. *Bunga raya* was the Malay name for hibiscus. Amazing what useless information the brain decided to store in its memory, while other, important matters were lost forever.

There was movement in the shade of the overhang above the steps to Justin's house. He came leaping down the stairs and marched down the path with long, easy strides. He was an attractive man, lean in hip and wide in shoulder. The still boyish looks of ten years ago had matured nicely, she thought. Three years he'd been here. A lonely life, she imagined. Of course, it was wasy enough to go to Penang now and then and enjoy the pleasures of more developed resort island. But Justin didn't seem the jet-set swinger type.

Justin didn't see her until he was close to the rain tree. He stopped, resting his hands easily on his hips.

'Had a swim already?'

'Just a short one. Didn't want to burn to a crisp my first day here.' And burning she did easily with her fair skin, although she could usually manage to get a light tan if she was careful and kept applying the lotion.

He frowned suddenly, came a step closer and peered at her thigh. 'What is that on your leg?'

She swallowed. 'A bruise.'

'It's a beaut. What did you do?' He lowered himself next to her in the shade.

'I fell against a coffee table.' Her voice sounded odd and she noticed the sharp look he gave her. Always those watchful eyes that seemed to see everything, probing.

'How did you fall?'

I tripped over a rug, a shoe. It was dark. I couldn't see well. She looked away. 'Somebody hit me and I lost my balance.'

There was a moment of heavy silence.

'Somebody hit you,' he repeated softly. 'May I guess who?'

Linden shrugged, still not looking at him.

'Did he hurt you?'

'Just a swollen lip. It didn't last long.'

'Was that the first time?'

She looked at him then, seeing the frowning forehead and the disturbed look in the dark eyes. 'You'd better believe it!' she said with soft vehemence in her voice. And the anger was back, curling hot in her stomach. 'Once is too often! I wasn't going to sit around and wait for a repeat!'

'So that's why you're here.' He was playing with a piece of white coral, forearms leaning on his raised knees, still observing her.

'I couldn't stay. He was the head of the Art Department in my college and I saw him every day. I knew I could not cope with that.'

'Why did he hit you?' He looked away, staring out over the ocean as he asked the question.

'He just lost control. He had a foul temper. There's something wrong with him. He had terrible black moods and it was getting worse and worse. In the end he hit me. That's where I got off the boat.' She was amazed at how calmly she spoke, but when she looked down on her hands she noticed they were tightly clasped together and the knuckles were white.

He did not reply and they were both silent.

After a while she came to her feet, shook the sand out of the towel and wrapped it around herself. 'I'll have to get a sarong,' she said lightly. 'As a matter of fact, I'd better make a list and do some more shopping. Are the shops open again around five?'

'Yes.' He leaped to his feet too. 'Let me know if you need help with anything.'

'Thanks.'

For a moment his eyes held hers. 'You've grown up,' he said quietly.

'Ten years will do that to a girl.' There was faint bitterness in her voice. *Ten years and a man like Waite,* she added silently.

As she walked back to the house she wondered how much he remembered of those two days he'd spent on the island those many years ago. And for what reasons he had come back here, of all places.

Nazirah was in the kitchen washing plates and cups and glasses and pots and pans when Linden came back. She went into the bathroom, washed off sand and sea water and shampooed her hair. It would take a while to dry without a hair dryer, but no matter. She had all the time in the world here. All the time she wanted for painting and reading. At home she never had time enough. Everything she wanted was here: time and peace and quiet. Simple surroundings. Good food. Sun and sand and sea and whispering palms. Solitude.

It's what she needed now—solitude. To forget and let the pain fade and the wounds heal. She sat on the verandah in a creaky rattan chair and brushed her wet hair. Drops of water dripped on her bare legs. Birds twittered in the trees, the only sound in the heavy, torpid heat of midday. Nothing moved, and the stillness almost seemed unreal. One of the palms close by had a heavy load of ripe green coconuts hanging in a cluster from its centre. They'd have to be cut down soon.

She was thirsty. In the kitchen she found a drink of water. It was cool and clean and came from the hand-dug well behind the house. She examined the refrigerator. It seemed in fine condition, but she wondered if it would still work, after three years. Maybe she should check with Justin.

The heat made her feel languid and drowsy. She lay down on the bed and for a while she slept.

At five she went into the village, bought tea and coffee, bread, mosquito coils, a green sarong, and a pineapple. Going from small shop to small shop, she examined the merchandise—aluminium cookware, balloons, comics in Malay, plastic buckets and crates of Coca Cola. A bald-headed westerner walked slowly down the street ahead of her. He had a pot belly and a limp. He wore shorts and a shirt and thongs. He was probably one of Justin's renters. A writer? An old colonial? A member of the Mafia? It would be interesting to find out, interesting to know why people came to this little island.

The three-legged yellow cart at the end of the shopping street seemed familiar. The face of the Chinese owner was familiar too when Linden came closer. Mak Long Teh, wearing baggy pants and a loose blouse. Still there selling her bowls of noodles and vegetables and shrimp, fried quickly in a wok over a kerosene burner. Linden stopped at the cart and smiled.

'Mak Long Teh! *Apa khabar?* How are you?'

The woman looked at Linden in surprise, then her eyes lit up and her face broke into a smile. Whoever thought the Chinese looked inscrutable had never been to Malaysia, Linden thought as she shook Mak Long Teh's hand.

'You have come back!' the woman said.

'I got hungry for your *mee goreng.*'

Mak Long Teh laughed her deep gurgling laugh. 'Is there no *mee goreng* in America?'

'Not like yours, Mak Long Teh.'

Mak Long Teh's eyes shone. 'Would you like some now?' Swiftly she began to cook the food, adding more shrimp than she would normally have, Linden noticed. As Linden ate, standing next to the cart with the bowl in her hand, Mak Long Teh told her about her family, about her daughter who had married and had recently had her first baby, and about her son who'd gone to Penang and worked as a waiter in the Casuarina Hotel restaurant.

It was dark when Linden walked back home,

carrying her purchases in plastic bags. Crickets chirped in the grass. A cool breeze blew in from the ocean and the sound of waves washing ashore sounded peaceful in the dark.

Nazirah had gone home. Linden lit the two kerosene lamps and brewed a cup of coffee. She sat down outside on the verandah, a mosquito coil beside her chair, and watched the darkened sea.

She sat there for a long time, feeling the loneliness seep through her, seeing Waite's face, hearing his voice, wishing he was with her to enjoy the peace of this place, to hold her in his arms and love her.

Don't think about Waite, she said to herself. *Don't think about Waite.*

It rained during the night and the sound of it awoke her. Wind blew hard through the palm trees and one of the shutters in the house was banging in the wind. With her sarong around her she went in search of it and closed it. She left the shutters open in her room and the air grew cool, almost chilly. The windows were mosquito-screened, had shutters, but no glass. Lying on the lumpy kapok mattress, she drew the sheet close around her and looked at the angry sky. It's like camping, she thought, lying in a tent so close to wind and rain, yet staying dry. Camping. Don't think about camping.

She forced her mind to concentrate on other things. The wind calmed down and the rain changed to a slow, steady drip that softly rustled the leaves and lulled her to sleep.

Several weeks went by. It rained a lot and the weather was cool. Her house was organised. The fridge was humming contentedly. She was getting used to living without electricity and running water. At night she went to bed early. No television to keep her a long awake. She woke up early every morning and went for walk along the beach or for a swim in the ocean. Then she'd have coffee and some breakfast and went into the village to buy her supply of food for the day. The vegetables in the *pasar* were freshly picked and beautiful. Nazirah cooked her a hot lunch and went home afterwards. Linden liked having the place to herself and she fixed her own dinner or went into the village to eat.

Every morning, after she returned from the market, she painted. A village carpenter had made her an easel and a stool, and she'd brought a supply of paints and canvas with her. The light inside the house was not very good, and often she worked outside in the yard, or on the verandah, with pots of paint, brushes, rags and turpentine next to her on a small table.

Her life took on a different rhythm, but the dull ache of loss stayed with her, haunting her all through her days and nights. She missed Waite. She missed his charm and warmth and loving. She missed his arms around her and the feeling of her head on his chest. Without love life seemed so empty. Sometimes she'd find herself staring at the painting, seeing nothing but his face and all she wanted to do was sink to the floor and cry her eyes out.

She wondered sometimes if coming to Pelangi Island had been a good idea. She was alone too much. There was too much time to think, too much loneliness that easily filled itself with doubts and uneasy thoughts. She began to doubt herself and her motivations. If she truly loved Waite, should she not forgive him? Had she really done enough to help him? Should she not stand by him? He was a man in trouble and he needed her. The questions churned inside her and at night she lay awake for hours at a time arguing with herself.

She was not happy with her work. It had lost its characteristic glow and liveliness, and seemed to reflect more and more her inner gloom and restlessness. She hated the colours, but somehow they found their way on to the canvas as if she had no control over them. She thought of Waite and his gloomy paintings and wondered fearfully what was happening to her.

Sometimes, in angry frustration, she'd throw down her brush and go for a walk on the beach. She'd climb the rocks and stare out over the water or watch the little crabs that scuttled between the rocks.

Now and then Justin would stop by, usually in the late afternoon, when the shadows were growing long and the light was softening to gold. She would offer tea and curry puffs or some other snack, delivered every day by a boy on a bicycle, and they'd talk for a while about nothing in particular, the conversation wandering here and there, never touching personal or intimate issues. Maybe that first day too much had been said too soon. Keeping distance was easier.

Sometimes they'd go for a swim in the late afternoon when the heat of day had faded. They'd watch the sun sink like a red ball of fire behind the horizon, streaking the sky lavender and violet and pale peach. The colours of water and sand and rock lost their brilliance in the waning light, became softer and subdued.

She was not always comfortable with him on the beach. His eyes were on her more than seemed necessary. A swimsuit or bikini hid very little and under his regard she felt less than adequately covered. He was not offensive, not in any way she could say, but she was aware of the desire in his eyes and it made her uneasy.

Now and then he'd ask her to go with him in his boat and she enjoyed that more than anything. She liked the sea at the end of the afternoon. The cool breeze felt good against her skin and she experienced a sense of peace and freedom out on the open water.

'May I see your paintings?' he asked one afternoon

as they were drinking glasses of chrysanthemum tea on her verandah.

She hesitated. She'd purposely hidden her paintings in the empty bedroom, not wanting him to see them. 'I've not been very happy with what I've done lately. I don't know what's wrong.'

'Don't you?' he asked, looking into her eyes. 'Of course you do.'

It was the closest they'd come in mentioning the reason for her stay here since the day she'd arrived. She looked down into her glass. 'I wish I knew what to do about it. I love painting, but lately I've been so frustrated, I feel like giving it up.'

'You can't, and you won't. You know that. You just have to keep going. Get it all out of your system.'

'I suppose you're right. I can't really imagine not painting ever again.' She stood up. 'I'll show you if you like. Just don't be too critical. My ego has been a little shaky lately.'

He came to his feet and stood very close, almost touching, and there was a strange light in his eyes. 'You're not blaming yourself, are you?' he asked, and there was quiet anger in his voice.

Blaming herself for Waite's violence? She shook her head. 'No.' She stepped back, uneasy with his nearness, and he followed her into the bedroom where she kept her supplies and finished work.

'I'm not an expert on painting,' he said, as he studied the canvasses, 'but I see what you mean.'

'What do you see?'

'Sadness. Frustration. Anger. I see it in the lines and especially in the colour.' He turned to look at her. 'But the work is good. Not an amateur by a long shot, are you?'

She gave a doubtful smile and turned to leave the room. He was nice to have around, undemanding. She liked talking with him.

'Come and have dinner with me tonight,' he said. 'I invited one of my renters; the old jogger. An interesting character. I think you'll enjoy him.'

'Oh, yes, I saw him on the beach yesterday.' He was an Englishman in his sixties, ramrod straight and tall, with a long grey moustache and a sharp, aristocratic nose. Apparently he jogged every morning to keep in condition, along with doing calisthenics before he went out. He'd been on the island for a week now and Linden had seen him around a few times.

She arrived early, wearing a long, green cotton skirt and a black, V-necked top. There was nothing fancy or expensive about her clothes, but they fit well and the colours looked good. She'd left her hair loose, the left side swept away from her face and fastened with an old tortoise-shell comb that had belonged to her grandmother. Justin's eyes ran over her quickly as he let her in, but in the dim shadows of the doorway she could not see his expression.

'Sit down, have a drink,' Justin invited. He looked trim and fit in his khaki pants and dark blue shirt. He was good to look at; she liked the way he moved, with the calm, easy movements of someone who's at peace with himself and the world. 'What would you like? Nothing sophisticated though—the bar is limited.' He gave a lopsided smile.

'How about a gin and tonic?'

'Can do.'

There was a *batek* painting on the wall and she crossed the room to stand in front of it. A scene of fishing boats—trawlers and smaller, brightly painted *prahus*. 'It's a Teng,' she said in delighted surprise. She'd once met the old man, a *batek* painter of international fame, trained in China. Exhibitions all over the world, a birthday card for Unicef, murals in Canberra and Kuala Lumpur, works hanging in private and public collections in many places.

'Yes.' He handed her the glass and stood next to her. 'Have you ever been to the Yahong Gallery at Batu Ferringhi?'

'Oh yes, many times. I met him there once. Talked to him for a quite a while. What's his full name again? Chuah something Teng.'

'Chuah Thean Teng.'

'Yes. He has a fantastic colour range, have you noticed? And I like his versatility. There was something different every time I went there. There's so much life and excitement in his work.' She sighed. 'He must be old by now?'

'Seventy, I think.'

She peered closer at the painting, examining the detail of colour and line. 'The intricacy always amazes me when you consider he works with wax and dye. I don't think I could ever learn.'

There was a knock on the door and they both looked up.

'Good evening.' Mr Courtney stood in the open door, tall, straight and smiling. He was dressed in white slacks, white socks, white leather shoes and a dark shirt. His grey hair and his bright blue eyes contrasted sharply with his tanned face. He entered on Justin's invitation and shook hands with Linden, eyes twinkling with delight at the sight of her.

Justin poured him a drink. Mr Courtney settled himself in a chair, shifting a little until he was perfectly comfortable, ready for the evening. He smoothed his long grey moustache.

'How is the writing going?' he asked Justin. 'Any more problems with the Bangkok connection?'

Justin handed him a Scotch. 'No. Your idea worked very well.' He turned to Linden. 'I was having trouble with a character and Mr Courtney gave me some advice.'

The old man laughed. 'That character reminded me of a RAF colonel I used to fly with in World War Two when I was stationed in Ceylon—Sri Lanka nowadays.' He put his drink down, smoothed his moustache again and leaned back, eager to tell the story.

Out came a hair-raising tale about a plane crash above the Indian Ocean in a driving rainstorm, of Mr Courtney and two others floating around for three days in a leaky rubber raft, each taking a turn keeping a finger over the hissing valve to prevent the air from escaping. A tale full of disasters, of the raft capsizing in the seething waves, of Mr Courtney's cigarettes and matches—stashed under his hat for safekeeping—getting soaked by sea water, of finally coming ashore and being greeted by police pointing 1895 rifles because fishermen had told them the Japanese were landing.

Linden watched him as he talked, seeing the laughter in his eyes, marvelling at his sense of humour as he spoke about his frightening adventures. He gestured as he spoke, shaking his head now and then as if he couldn't quite believe he had survived the ordeal. He must have told the story a hundred times, but his enthusiasm for telling it seemed not to have waned.

It took a long time to eat dinner. Garrulous Mr Courtney had more than one story. 'That reminds me,' he'd say, putting down his fork and smoothing his moustache, and another story would follow.

Linden asked him what he had done after the war. He had stayed on in Ceylon, running a coconut estate, work for which the RAF had not prepared him. He had married and raised a family. His children were grown now and his wife had died. He was alone now and it was easy to see how he enjoyed reminiscing about his past.

Over after-dinner coffee he entertained them with a story about the ghost of an old man that appeared in his bedroom one night when he stayed in the house of a friend in the hills in Ceylon.

'The next morning at breakfast, my friend said, "Oh, by the way, did you meet Harry?" And I said, "Harry? Who's Harry?" "Harry's the old man that comes into your room at night. I forgot to tell you about him. He's quite harmless you know. He's done it for years."' Mr Courtney laughed. 'I didn't sleep in that room again. I might be English, but I don't like to mix with ghosts.' He finished his coffee and came to his feet. 'Well, young people, I must go. Thank you very much for a delightful evening.'

'I enjoyed that,' said Linden after Mr Courtney had gone and sighed with contentment. 'The food almost as much as the company. He's a great old goat, as my friend Liz would say. Well, I should be going too.' She stood up.

'What's your hurry? There's some wine left. Why don't we finish it?'

Well, why not? There was nothing but an empty house to go back to, and she didn't feel particularly sleepy. She sat down again. 'All right, thanks.'

She watched him as he poured the wine. 'You seem so serious all the time,' she said off the top of her head, her tongue loosened by the good food and wine. 'I remember you as a joker and a laugher. But then, that was ten years ago.'

'Ten years is a long time.'

He said no more and she didn't want to pry. 'Are you planning to settle down here? For a long time, I mean.'

'I don't think so. It's about time to think about going back home again.'

'You seem to like it here.'

'It's peaceful. The people are happy. They don't go hungry and there is no war.' Something flickered in his eyes as he spoke, and she felt a tightening of her chest.

'What did you do before you came to Pelangi?'

'I was a war correspondent in Beirut, hanging out in the Commodore Hotel in the Hamra waiting for the next car bomb to go off.'

It was not at all what she had expected and it started

all manner of thoughts and ideas in her mind. Calm quiet Justin in a war-ridden country doing dangerous work—it seemed so out of character. Or was it? She'd known there had been more to him than his quiet, aloof manner gave away, something hidden behind that impassive face.

'Not such a peaceful place, Lebanon.'

'No. And I was young and stupid. I wandered the streets and was in places I shouldn't have been. It's a jungle out there. Everybody is everybody's enemy. To make a long story short, I got caught in cross fire and got shot in the back. I was lucky I didn't die. They patched me up and shipped me back to the States. I spent months in the hospital. Lying there I decided I'd had enough and to recuperate I was going to find the most peaceful place I could think of.'

'And you thought of Pelangi.'

'At first it seemed a crazy idea, but the more I thought about it the more I wanted to come here. I'd wanted for a long time to try my hand on fiction writing, and this seemed like the ideal opportunity. I decided to write a spy novel and see what happened after that.'

He had stayed and written another one. And here he was, writing his fourth, with a New York editor eager for more. He'd spent some time in Bangkok, Hong Kong and Singapore, doing research. For the rest of the time he stayed on Pelangi with the exception of a trip to Penang now and then.

Several times friends had come to stay with him on the island, and the idea of building one or two more small fishermen's houses for other peace-seekers was born. It gave him something to do besides staring at the typewriter all day, and the colourful characters that came and visited were a welcome diversion and sometimes good writing material.

'Like Mr Courtney,' he said. 'I've been squeezing him like a mop, only he doesn't know it. At least I think not.' His lips curled down in something that resembled a smile.

'You don't actually write about real people, do you?'

'No, of course not. I use them for raw material only, using bits and pieces in different places. It's never recognisable. You have to make the characters fit the story, so usually it's quite impossible to use a ready-made person.'

'I'd like to read one of your books, if you don't mind. I don't usually read spy stories, so I don't know much about the genre, but . . .'

He got up out of his chair and took a book off the shelf. 'Here, try this one. It's the latest.'

The cover was black with a picture of a Chinese temple in red and gold, and a long-haired blonde with a gun in her hand in the foreground. She wore a minimum of clothes and had a desperate look in her eyes.

'Some picture,' Linden commented, and he groaned.

'The covers are terrible, in my opinion, but I assume the publisher knows what the public wants.'

'Half-naked blondes and guns,' she countered drily. 'Well, I must be going.' She stood up. 'Oh, by the way, how gory is this? If I start reading it now, will it keep me awake?'

He gave a crooked little grin. 'I hope so.'

She grimaced in embarrassment. 'Sorry, I didn't mean it that way. I wasn't referring to its entertainment value. But blood and gore gives me nightmares.'

'No blood and gore. Just a couple of nice clean killings. That's all.'

'Oh, well, I can handle a couple of clean killings.'

They were standing near the door, smiling at each other and suddenly something was different—the atmosphere seemed strangely charged and he looked at her in a way he had not done before. In slow motion his hand moved up and touched her hair and the breath caught in her throat. For an endless moment their eyes were locked and time stood still. She saw his face coming closer, and she backed away, not knowing why, just moved away from him. Her heart was like a wild thing trapped in her chest and breathing was difficult.

'I have to go. Good night, Justin.' She had to force out the words. She turned, took a step down the stairs and almost stumbled. He grabbed her arm to steady her.

'I'll walk you home.' He stood behind her, still holding on to her arm.

Let go of me! Don't touch me! The words screamed in her head, but her tongue made no sound. Moving away from his touch, she rushed down the remaining few steps, her heart thundering and her breathing fast. He followed her into the night and silently they walked the short distance to her house. The air was warm and fragrant. The sky clear and speckled with stars. It had rained earlier in the afternoon and the earth was damp and moisture still clung to the bushes and trees. Insects buzzed in the greenery and some nocturnal creature chirped eerily in the dark.

Only a few kerosene lamps burned in the village. Most people had gone to bed hours ago. It was too dark to see his face, but she was aware of his bulk and his nearness as they stood at the bottom of the steps to her door.

'Thanks very much for dinner,' she said turning to go up the steps. 'Good night.'

'Good night, Linden.' He took off with long strides, down the path back to his house.

Linden opened the door and went in, lit a lamp and took it into the bedroom. Slowly she took off her clothes, watching on the wall the contorted shadows her movements made. Why had she reacted so strangely? What was wrong with Justin kissing her?

Why such a strong reaction? She felt the tenseness in her body and wondered what was happening to her.

She walked into the bathroom, naked, and scooped water from a bucket and splashed it over her, gasping with the cold shock of it on her warm skin. She took a deep breath, poured more water over her and it felt good and cool, no longer cold.

There was a long narrow mirror in her room, attached to the door. She looked at her bare body, finding herself too thin and too pale. The bruise on her thigh had faded. She thought of Waite, holding her. She thought of his gentle, sensitive fingers and her stomach cramped in pain and tears stung her eyes. She lay in bed, curled up into a ball, tight with aching longing. She wanted somebody with her, someone to touch her and caress her and make her feel wanted and loved. Somebody, anybody to fill this horrible void of loneliness.

But Justin had touched her and she'd withdrawn. He had wanted to kiss her and she had backed away. She didn't want just anybody. She wanted Waite. *No! Not Waite!* Not ever again Waite. He had hit her, hurt her, bruised her mouth and walked out on her. She could not let him touch her again, not ever again.

She thought of Justin kissing her, his hands moving over her body, making love to her. She jerked upright in bed, flinging her hair out of her face. *No! No!* She stumbled out of bed, tied the sarong around her and slowly found her way to the verandah, holding on the walls so as not to fall in the dark. She sat in the dark staring out over the sea until the mosquitoes found her and began to attack her ankles. She found her thongs by the door and carefully went down the stairs. It was not far to the beach and her eyes were used to the dark by now.

She took off her thongs when she reached the beach and slogged through the coarse sand to the water's edge and waded in ankle deep to get some relief from her itchy bites. The sea was quiet, with calm subdued little waves that broke close to the beach. Definitely not a surfer's paradise, this, she thought. Taking deep breaths of the tangy sea air, she felt herself calm down.

'I'll get over this,' she said out loud to herself. 'I'm not the only one with a broken heart in this world.'

As she made her way back to the house, she noticed a light still burning in Justin's house. Was he reading in bed? Or working? Then she remembered the book he had given her and she lit the lamp again and, sitting up in bed, began to read.

When she awoke it was seven and somewhere close by her window a bird chirped joyously and insistently. The kerosene lamp had burned itself out and the book had slid off the bed on to the floor. Picking it up she found where she had stopped reading and realised she'd finished more than half. She yawned, still exhausted, and cursed the loud little bird outside her window.

There were soft sounds from the kitchen and she realized that Nazirah had already arrived and was cleaning. Linden dragged herself out of the bed and wrapped the sarong around her. Opening the door slightly, she called out to Nazirah, who came at a run.

'Would you make me some coffee, please, Nazirah? And a slice of bread and honey?'

'Are you ill?' The girl looked worried. Linden was always up when she arrived and to find her in bed was cause for concern.

Linden shook her head. 'I couldn't sleep last night. I'm still tired.'

She ate the bread and drank the coffee sitting up in bed. Then, having decided against getting up, she half-closed the shutters against the bright morning light and curled up under the sheet again. An hour later she woke up again, feeling better.

After more coffee, she decided to go for a hike in the

hills, go up to the waterfalls and finish Justin's book. Nazirah packed a small backpack with a thermos of cold water, some cold chicken and sliced pineapple. Linden stuffed in the book, a sketch pad, a towel and her sarong. Dressed in shorts, a shirt, and plimsolls, she set off.

She had to go through the village, past the shops and the *pasar*, and the curious looks she received were beginning to annoy her. It was her own fault. She shouldn't have worn shorts, or at least should have covered them up with a sarong. Oh, well. The thing was tucked away in her backpack and she'd just have to keep on going. She passed a butcher on wheels—a motorcycle with a screened box built on the back. Inside the contraption chunks of meat hung from small hooks waiting for customers. Mak Long Teh stood at the end of the street with her yellow *gerai* and Linden called out a greeting to her. Outside the village she passed the smoke house where wood was burned into charcoal—enough to supply the village.

For a while she walked along the narrow unpaved road, meeting only an occasional cyclist or woman carrying a load on her back. The scenery was breathtaking, with rice paddies terraced on the slopes of the hills and clumps of coconut trees and banana plants here and there. Women wearing conical hats were working in the fields, bending over as they weeded the rice. Finally she reached the narrow path that led into the hills up to the waterfalls.

There was no hurry and she went slowly, climbing steadily up the narrow jungle path along the stream that started up higher in the hills. The path was overgrown because not many people followed the stream up that far. Down below, where it reached the village, the women came to do their washing and the children played and bathed in it.

There were small waterfalls up above and a rocky pool that formed a natural bathing place. The water was cool and clean and babbled and rushed among the boulders. She remembered the blissful feeling of swimming there naked, alone in this green, serene paradise with only the butterflies and the birds and an occasional monkey for company.

It was to this place that she had taken Justin so many years ago, where she had flirted with him so unashamedly. Now, as she climbed the path in the dappled sunshine, she laughed at the memory of it, at the girl she had been then—so young and romantic and so eager for love.

Halfway up, she stopped to have a drink of water. Sitting on a large, smooth rock in the shade of a thick clump of bamboo ten feet tall, she took in the scenery and sighed with the beauty of it. Vines with white and purple blooms wound their ways around tree trunks. Bushes with bright pink and orange and yellow flowers of the most delicate shapes grew wild along the path. A large, brown and white butterfly fluttered past. In a tree nearby a bird made a high, warbling sound.

Again, unbidden, the thought was in her mind. *Waite would enjoy this.*

Don't think about Waite.

She screwed the cup back on to the thermos and put it in the pack. How did you not think of someone who'd been the centre of your life for two years? Someone you'd seen and talked to and been with almost every day?

Some of the joy had gone out of her hike. She climbed on, feeling hot now and wet with perspiration.

When finally she reached the waterfalls, her face was flushed and her heart was pumping with the exertion. Dropping the pack off her back on to the ground, she sat down on a tree trunk. She unlaced her plimsolls and took off her socks. Her feet were hot. She wiggled her toes and stretched her legs out into the sun. The water gurgled and splashed as it fell over the ledges into the rocky basin. The water looked cool and inviting. She lifted her tee-shirt over her head and took it off. Then her bra, and shorts. She stood, hesitating, wearing only her red panties, and looked around. There wasn't a soul for miles around. She stripped off the panties too, tossing them on to her heap of clothes on a large flat rock. Raising her arms high above her head, she stretched in the sun, feeling suddenly free and gloriously alive and the joy was back. She laughed out loud and pirouetted on one foot, feeling a warm breeze caress her bare skin and she lifted her face to the sky and felt the sun warm upon it. She laughed again, then looked down on the ground and tiptoed carefully to the water.

The water was icy cold as she slipped into it and the breath caught in her throat. Goosepimples covered her arms and legs and it took a moment before she could breathe normally again and the worst of the cold eased from her limbs. She swam around the small pool, kicking and splashing with vigour to keep her circulation going. After a while she felt no longer cold and a sense of well-being pervaded her.

Later she sat on a rock, letting the sun dry her. She unbraided her hair and shook it loose to let it dry too. It would take a long time for it was thick and heavy and hung down to the middle of her back.

When the sun became too hot she spread the towel and the sarong out on the ground for padding and lay down in the shade to read. Turning from back to stomach she read for two hours straight through until the book was finished. It was exciting and fascinating and held her attention till the last page. Still, there was something about it that bothered her.

It was a good, fast-moving story, a lot of action, which she assumed appealed to male readers, and had an interesting hero. But something was missing. There was something wrong with the hero. He was a sharp, humorous man who acted purely on logic and reason.

There was no feeling in the man, no emotion. He did not get upset or angry or sad or desperate. She sighed and laid the book aside, her eyes catching the cheap cover design. The beautiful woman had loved him and even her he had treated coldly and selfishly.

She had another drink of water and bit hungrily into a piece of chicken. Having finished her lunch, the taste of pineapple still sweet in her mouth, she lay down again and sighed contentedly. The air was warm even in the shade. Closing her eyes, she listened to the noises around her, the rushing water, the birds and the insects and the breeze rustling the leaves.

When she opened her eyes she was no longer alone.

Justin was sitting not far from her in the shade and was looking at her, his mouth faintly curling at the corners.

'Eve in the Garden of Eden,' he said softly. 'Very nice.'

CHAPTER THREE

FOR a moment she didn't move, just stared at him silently. Then heat suffused her. She didn't know if it was anger or embarrassment or both. Leaping to her feet, she turned her back to him, yanked the sarong off the ground and wrapped it around herself.

He had as much right to be here as she did. Yet she felt as if he had intruded on her private domain. She must have fallen asleep or she would have heard him coming. How long had he been there looking at her? Well, he'd probably seen the odd naked female in his life.

She sat down on the towel, crosslegged and silent, and began to brush out her hair. It was still far from dry and was full of knots. She must look like an ugly witch.

'You fell asleep reading my book?' It was a question without accusation.

'I was finished,' she said curtly, yanking at her hair. Oh, damn, she thought, I should just cut it all off.

'I get the impression you're not overjoyed to see me,' he said conversationally.

'I wasn't dressed for visitors.'

'That all depends on how you look at it,' he said evenly.

'Oh, shut up!' She threw down the brush, grabbed her clothes off the rock and looked around for a place to change.

'Hey!' He leaped to his feet, stood in front of her and looked into her eyes, frowning. 'What's the matter with you all of a sudden?'

She gave him a vicious look and turned away from him without answering. He took her shoulders in an iron grip and turned her back.

'I was asking you a question,' he said softly. 'Now answer me. What is wrong? What did I do?'

'Nothing. Now let go of me!'

He didn't. 'It started last night, didn't it? You didn't want me to kiss you.'

She stared right into his eyes. 'Right.'

His expression didn't change. 'Well,' he said quietly, 'I like you. I'm attracted to you. I like to be with you and talk to you. Last night I wanted to kiss you. Is that so bad?'

She took a deep breath. 'All right, let me make this clear to you. This is not a good time for me. I'm not in the mood for romance. I don't want it.' She looked at him hard, her body rigid under his hands on her shoulders. They felt warm and strong on her bare skin and she swallowed painfully.

He lifted one hand and trailed his fingers through her damp hair. 'When?' he asked quietly.

'What do you mean, when?'

'When will you be in the mood again? I remember you here in this very same place a long time ago.' There was the faintest flicker of humour in his eyes. 'You were very much in the mood then.'

Linden sighed in frustration. 'Oh, for God's sake! I was a child. Silly, romantic, wearing rose-coloured glasses.'

'Yes,' he agreed. 'And now you're no longer a child.' He took his hands away and she turned to go.

'Don't leave, Linden. Have a swim.'

'I already did.'

'Well, have another one.'

'No. I'm going.' She went behind some bushes and pulled on her clothes. Then she stuffed her things into the backpack, sat down again and began to braid her hair while Justin watched her silently. Finished, she slung the pack on her back and slipped her arms through the straps.

'Wait,' he said suddenly, fishing around in his back pocket. 'I have a letter for you.'

'A letter?'

'They gave it to me at the post office.' He handed it to her. 'I came to your house to give it to you and Nazirah told me you'd gone on a hike to the waterfalls. It seemed like a good idea.'

She took the letter from him, sliding the pack back to the ground. It was from Liz. Linden sat back down on the rock and ripped it open and began to read. Liz had found someone to sub-let Linden's apartment, which was a relief. She was using her savings to pay the rent—she'd been hesitant in letting go of the place. She read on:

> *Waite is frantic, he's been to see me several times now trying to find out where you are. I keep telling him I don't know, but he doesn't believe me. Well, he isn't stupid, is he? He looks awful. He's suffering badly. He loves you, you know.*

She lowered the letter to her knees and looked blindly ahead, tears filling her eyes. Her throat ached with the effort not to cry and she swallowed hard and painfully. But suddenly the grief was too overwhelming and she found the sobs rising in her. Hastily stuffing the letter in her pack she got up and walked off into the shady greenery, sat down on a fallen tree trunk and cried till her body ached.

He was pouring coffee from a thermos when she came back. 'Have some,' he said, handing her a cup. She took it without a word and sat down again near the rocky pool, not looking at him. She felt washed out from her crying. She knew she looked red-eyed and awful, but she didn't care. Taking the towel from her pack, she dipped one end into the water and held it against her face. The cold was a shock against her heated face, but it felt good.

'What's his name?' Justin asked.

'Waite.'

'Looked like a woman's handwriting on the envelope.'

'It was. A letter from my friend. Waite doesn't know I am here.'

They sipped their coffee.

'Would you like a sandwich?'

'No thanks. I had my lunch.' She turned to look at him. He bit into a sandwich, the bread almost disappearing into his big brown hand.

'Why weren't you writing this morning?' she asked.

He shrugged, chewed and swallowed. 'Didn't do so well this morning. I was at the typewriter at six, but didn't produce much. I had trouble with the lady in the story. I didn't feel like fighting it, so I gave up and gave myself a day off.'

'In the book I just finished, Max was in love with the French girl, right?'

'Yes.'

'Why didn't he show it? He was so cold.'

He stared at her. 'You thought so?'

'Yes. He was an interesting character, except that I thought he was much too selfish.'

'In what way?'

Linden shrugged. 'He used her. He took for granted she was always waiting for him when he came back. When she made demands of her own, he waved them away. He didn't want to bother himself with her wishes. He really didn't even want to consider them.'

'It wasn't the right time in his life for a permanent relationship.' His mouth quirked. 'He was too busy spying.'

'Not fair to the girl, though.'

'No, not fair at all.'

She caught something in his voice and their eyes met for a fleeting moment.

'Is that what happened to you?' she asked. 'Too busy running around the world covering wars and revolutions?'

The dark eyes looked at her intently. 'You're very perceptive.'

'It wasn't difficult to guess.'

'Well, it's a long time ago.' He took another bite of his sandwich. He had stripped off his shirt and was sitting in the sun. His chest was very brown and contrasted sharply with his white shorts. His legs were strong and muscled and the dark hair glinted in the sun. Above the waistband of his shorts she noticed a scar on his left side.

'What happened there?' she asked, pointing at it.

'Another battle scar. El Salvador, Central America, another garden spot.'

'Good Lord, where else have you been?'

'I try not to remember.' He took another bite of his sandwich. Obviously this was not a welcome topic of conversation.

She finished her coffee and gave him back the cup. 'Thanks.' She slung the pack on her back and slid her arms through the straps. 'I'm off. See you.'

His mouth full of food, he gave a wave of his hand in goodbye.

The trail back to the village seemed endless and she trudged down the path, seeing and hearing nothing around her, feeling miserable.

She'd dragged her easel and paints and brushes out to the beach and was painting the rocks, the white clouds above them and the blue and orange trawler in the foreground. It was going well, better than in weeks. She lost herself in time, seeing only shape and form and line and colour, a magic place where nothing else mattered. So intently was she working that she didn't notice the man until he was standing near her.

She looked up sharply, irritated at the interruption. She'd not been able to let herself go like this for such a long time. Resentment burned inside her. It was like a rude awakening to be dragged back out of that curious sense of concentration to find someone standing there watching her work. He was about fifty, she guessed, short and broad-shouldered, with a dark, swarthy look, and sharp black eyes. Once he'd been handsome, but now he was flabby and out of shape. He wore a shirt and a sarong and was barefoot.

'Miss Mitchell?' He was looking her over, his eyes like a touch on her body. He made her skin crawl.

'Yes,' she answered coldly.

'My name is Julio Marinozzi. Justin spoke of you.' His dark eyes were now trained on the painting. 'Excellent,' he commented. 'Is it for sale?'

Resentment faded. She felt a stir of excitement, but was determined not to show it. 'It's not finished yet.'

'And when it is finished?'

She nodded. 'Yes.' There were more paintings stacked against the wall of the spare bedroom than she knew what to do with. Living on the island was extremely cheap, but not free, and without a regular paycheque she'd eventually run out of savings. The sale of one painting—if she got the price she got at home—would keep her for a couple of months on Pelangi.

Mr Marinozzi gave her a brilliant smile, white teeth flashing in his dark face. 'Good, good,' he said, hitching up his sarong. 'Let me know when it is finished and we will discuss the price. And now, let me not disturb you any longer. Good day.'

She watched him for a moment as he plodded off through the dry sand. The old lecher. Must be one of the renters, newly arrived, for she had not seen him before. She returned her attention to the painting, trying to look at it through objective eyes. It was good. The colours worked well together. It really was beautiful, and she felt a flush of joy. For a while she worked on, but her concentration had gone. The light was changing and she noticed the dark formation of thunder clouds on the horizon.

Packing up her things she went back to the house. It was later than she thought—almost lunch time. In the kitchen Nazirah was cooking curried shrimp and the spicy smell made her ravenous.

The sky turned ominously dark. Nazirah lit one of the kerosene lamps to use in the kitchen and put a couple of candles on the table for Linden.

The rain came while she was eating. It thundered down with a sudden, instant violence that always amazed her. One minute it was dry, the next the water came down in torrents. It poured from the heavens for about half an hour, then slowed down to a steady rain for another hour, then to a drizzle.

She went out on to the verandah. The world was wet and steaming. The trees dripped. Flowers drooped. Sodden frangipani blooms littered the soaked grass. The sky drooled a grey mist. A soft wind stirred the sodden greenery. Birds, hidden, chirped. Chickens and roosters pranced around in the mud. Puddles gleamed on the paths.

It was cool but not cold. She went out into the drizzle and strolled along the beach. The sea was grey and restless. She picked up some flat, round shells with a pearly shine, thin as glass. Some were pale silvery in colour, others shiny charcoal. She stuffed them in the pocket of her jeans to add to her collection. She was always picking up things, not knowing what to do with them, but wanting to take them home and look at them again.

She reached the rocks and sat down, inhaling the cool, wet sea air. Among the boulders small crab-like creatures scrambled in the current of ebb and flow of water, and for a while she watched them until she got bored.

It had stopped drizzling. She didn't feel like going home, so she went into the village and looked at the houses, the potted plants neatly arranged around them, the clean-swept yards, the laundry on lines underneath the houses. Children were out playing barefoot in the puddles. Five black and white ducks sat neatly in a row on a fallen tree trunk, twitching their feathers.

Justin was coming down the path as she reached her house again.

'Had a walk in the rain?' he asked, looking at her damp clothes.

'It's nice when it doesn't make you cold.' She shook her braid back over her shoulder. 'Were you coming to see me?' The incident at the waterfalls had not changed their routine. Justin still came to see her now and then, or asked her over for a drink in the evenings. The last few weeks had gone by quickly and calmly, but she had to admit that the solitude she initially had come looking for was beginning to bore her.

'You have time for coffee?'

She spread her arms wide. 'Oceans of time.'

He gave her a sharp look. 'Something wrong?'

'I think I'm bored. I'm beginning to think that television might be exciting.'

His smile was faint. 'Oh boy, you're in trouble.'

'Don't you ever get bored?'

'When I do I fly to Kuala Lumpur or Bangkok to visit friends. After a few days of that, Pelangi is like heaven again.'

'Well, maybe I should have a wild weekend in George Town. That is, if I sell my painting to Mr Italiano. What's his name?'

'Marinozzi. Julio. You've met him?'

'He approached me on the beach, took one look at a half finished painting and decided he wanted it.' She grinned. 'Of course he hasn't heard my price yet.'

'I wouldn't worry about it. If he wants it he'll pay anything.'

She grinned wider. 'Thanks for telling me that. The price just went up.'

Justin laughed. 'Quite the mercenary, aren't you?'

'Listen, it's been a while since I saw my last paycheque!'

'Sorry, sorry . . . didn't mean it.' His eyes were laughing. 'Put some dry clothes on if you want to have coffee with me. That wet tee-shirt is bad for my blood pressure.'

Involuntarily she looked down at her shirt, seeing it cling to her breasts, revealing them in all their detail.

'Eat your heart out,' she said, and rushed up the stairs to her house. She heard him laugh and she slammed the door closed. She wondered what was happening to him. He seemed to be less serious and more lighthearted lately, laughing and smiling more often.

He groaned when he saw her come into the door fifteen minutes later. 'Did you have to wear that sack?' he asked.

'What sack? This is not a sack. This is a caftan. Very exotic material, don't you see?' It covered her up from shoulder to ankle in wide folds of vivid blue, hiding every line and curve of her body.

'I'd rather see what's underneath it.'

'You've seen it all before.' She turned her back on him and examined the books on the shelves. 'I'd like to borrow some more books, please.'

He was behind her, turning her around to face him. His hands slid down her side and came to rest on her hips. She glared at him.

'Justin, I warn you. Get your hands off me.'

'I want to know it's really you underneath this thing.'

She could feel the warmth of his hands through the thin material. They moved up to her waist and she slapped them away. He put them next to her head against the bookshelf and looked into her eyes. Her heart began to race; there was nothing she could do about it. She felt uneasy under his gaze, but she was trapped with her back against the bookcase.

'There's a whole village of willing maidens out there. Why don't you pick on them?'

He shook his head. 'And ruin their reputations? Have a heart!'

She sighed. 'You're not worried about my reputation, I take it.'

He lifted one eyebrow. 'Are you?'

She grimaced, not answering.

'Why don't you relax? You might even like it.'

'I *have* been kissed before.'

'Ah, but not by me.'

'Oh, yes I have.'

For a moment he looked confused, then his expression cleared and he grinned. 'By the falls? That hardly counts. That was my gentleman's kiss for innocent girls. I assume you are no longer innocent.'

'Oh, shut up, Justin!' She pushed against his chest, but it was useless and she let her arms drop by her sides in defeat. 'What's got into you lately?'

'Don't ask dumb questions.' He lowered his arms and took both her hands in his. His hands were big and brown, but nicely shaped, holding on to her securely. Good hands, she thought, as if it mattered. She kept staring down at them, not pulling away.

'Look at me,' he said softly.

She was surprised at the sudden change in him, to see the look in his eyes. There was gentleness and warmth there, and the teasing laughter had gone. The tenseness inside subsided and when his lips touched hers she did not resist.

She closed her eyes and there was a warm melting sensation in her stomach. His lips were firm, parting hers and the taste and smell of him made her knees weak. He held her close against him and the blood rushed madly through her limbs, filling her with wild longings. It was wonderful and terrible and the force of it made her dizzy.

I don't want this! The thought exploded in her head.

I don't want this! She tore away with frantic strength and he let her go.

They looked at each other. There was silence, broken only by the rich warbling of a bird outside and the sound of the sea washing on to the beach.

She stood very still, willing her breathing to its normal rhythm. She swallowed, the taste of him still in her mouth.

'I would like that cup of coffee now.'

He nodded, turned and left the room. With unsteady legs she moved to a chair and sat down. He came back a moment later, strode up to the bookcase and took some books off the shelf.

'Have you read any Ken Follet? Or Wilbur Smith?'

She shook her head. 'No, I haven't.'

'Try Wilbur Smith. I'm sure you'll like him.' He handed her several and she looked at the titles, glad to have something to do. She felt uncomfortable, as if too much had been revealed and she could not bear to acknowledge it now by word or look.

The coffee was brought in by Ramayah, Justin's cook, an old woman with her hair pulled back from her face and sharp eyes that missed nothing. She entered the room, padding softly on bare feet, carrying a tray. She wore a sarong around her waist and a long-sleeved fitted blouse over it. Carefully she placed the coffee and the cups on the table, then a plate with friend bananas.

'Do you know,' he said after Ramaya had left, 'that Christmas is a week from today?'

'A week?' She'd lost all sense of time. In this tropical world it was not easy to think of Christmas. There were a few Chinese Christians on the island, but most of the islanders were Muslim, traditional Chinese or Hindu. 'I hadn't even thought of it,' she said.

'You're not going home for Christmas?'

'No. There's nothing there for me.' Her tone was flat.

'What about your sister?'

'Her family always spends Christmas with her parents-in-law. I'm welcome enough, but . . .' she shrugged. 'I don't feel very much at home there, and Stefanie always gets on my nerves.'

He raised one dark eyebrow. 'Why is that?'

'She thinks I should get married and have a dozen children. She has four herself and she's younger than I am. Married at eighteen. First baby at nineteen. Second a year later. Then a set of twins. And if that isn't enough, she's pregnant again. It makes me nervous just thinking of five kids under five.'

He gave a hearty laugh. 'Some people are happy with a lot of kids.'

'*She* is, and that's great. But she has this misguided notion that the rest of the world should feel just like she does. She hasn't caught on to the idea of freedom of choice. It's irritating. We always get into arguments.'

'What do you want for yourself?'

'Oh, I'd like a family—a couple of kids, but I'd still like time for my painting.'

'Were you planning to marry this man . . . Waite?'

She stabbed her fork in a piece of banana. 'We talked about it.'

'And?'

'I got scared.' In the end she hadn't even wanted to talk about it anymore. She put her plate down. 'Is there any more coffee?'

'Help yourself.'

She poured the coffee. 'You too?'

'Please.'

She took his cup and filled it. 'Did you ever think about getting married?'

'I was too busy.' He paused. 'And too selfish.'

There was a silence. 'What happened?' she asked softly.

He looked into his cup. 'Her name was Kate. We

were together for more than four years. I'd be gone for
months at a time, but when I'd come home we'd have
a wonderful time. In the beginning it worked out all
right. She had a demanding career of her own and was
very busy. But later she became unhappy with the
arrangement. She wanted to settle down, have a baby.'

'And you didn't want to?'

'I wasn't ready. I couldn't see why we couldn't go
on the way we had for the past years. It suited my life
very well. She was always there for me when I came
home. I was a selfish bastard.'

'What happened?'

'It went on for another year or so. I think she hoped
I'd change my mind, but I didn't. Then one time I
came home and she wasn't there.' He put the cup
down. 'I went crazy.'

'Did you find her?'

'Yes. But it was too late. Nothing could persuade
her to come back to me.' He paused. 'The next time I
was in Beirut I got shot. After that, in the hospital, I
had a lot of time to think.' He picked up his cup again,
staring into it without drinking. After a while he
leaned back in his chair and looked at her.

'Would you like to go to Penang for Christmas?
Stay in one of the hotels, have a nice dinner? My
treat.'

She didn't know what to say. She looked at him and
he slowly shook his head.

'No strings attached.'

It was wrong, and she knew it. She nodded. 'I'd like
that.'

For the next few days she worked on the painting and
when it was finished and dry she hung it on one of the
walls where the light was good.

Mr Marinozzi's house was behind Justin's and she
skipped up the stairs and stood in the open door. He
was sitting at the table and looked up from a stack of

computer printouts. He came to his feet immediately, smiling broadly.

'Please come in, Miss Mitchell.' He put a heavy arm around her shoulders and his touch made her shiver with revulsion. He led her to a chair. 'Sit down, sit down.'

She slipped away from under his arm and moved back to the door. She gestured at the table. 'You're working. I don't want to disturb you. I just came to tell you that the painting is finished and you can come by and see it.'

'It's finished? Good, good! But do sit down and have a drink.' He chuckled. 'I should not be working at all, actually—doctor's orders, you see, but working to me is like eating and sleeping and eh, well, never mind.'

'Thank you, but no, I must go.' It was an effort to stay civil. She didn't like this overgrown Don Juan. His smile was too oily for comfort and his hands too loose. He stood beside her near the door, much closer than necessary. Automatically she moved out on to the first step of the stairs, feeling at the same time his hand slide down her buttock. For a moment she was too outraged to react, then practically jumped down the stairs. *Ignore it, don't say a thing*, she told herself and forced herself to look up at him from the safety of the ground.

'If you have time, come by about five. I'll be home then.' And she'd ask Justin to come for a cold drink, just in case. No sense in taking any risks. She laughed to herself as she walked back home. Talk about risk. Justin was probably just as likely to go for her as this aging Latin lover.

But it all went as civilised as could be. He was truly enchanted by the painting, he said. A true piece of art, and that by someone so young and sweet. Behind his back Linden rolled her eyes at Justin, who sat back in his chair and winked at her.

'A young, sweet *professional*, sir,' she said smiling at him innocently. 'I hope too that you find the price sweet enough.' She mentioned an amount, twice as high as what she'd sold her last paintings for, and he did not blink an eye.

'Would you like that in cash or a cheque?'

'Cash, please, if you have it. It's easier here.'

He pulled out a bulging, snake-skin wallet. 'Malaysian dollars? If you prefer American dollars I can get those for you in a couple of days.'

'Malaysian dollars will be fine.' She couldn't believe what she was seeing. Who in this day and age went around with that kind of money in cash in his wallet? Hadn't the man heard of credit cards and travellers' cheques?

He counted out the notes on the coffee table while Linden looked on in amazement. She glanced over at Justin, who watched the proceedings impassively.

After Mr Marinozzi had left, the wrapped painting under his arm, Linden looked at Justin again and began to laugh softly. 'He had twice that much in his wallet.'

'He would probably have given it all if you'd asked for it.'

'That would be overdoing it a little.'

He shrugged. 'Why? The price of art is very elusive, you should know that. If it was worth that to him, then it was worth that.'

She looked at the pile of money on the table. 'I guess I'd better put that away in a sock. I don't have one. Do you have a sock?'

'What colour?'

She began to laugh again. 'Oh my, this is ridiculous.' She gathered up the money. 'Just a minute.' She put the bills in an old paint box and hid it in her clothes closet. Not a very good place, but in this little house there wasn't anything better.

'Well,' she said, coming back into the room, 'now I

can pay my own way on Penang. We can really live it up now.'

'Too late. You already agreed.'

'Oh, for heaven's sake! I had no money, Justin! Now I do.'

'Right. And you'd better hang on to it for a while. Being a sweet, young professional artist, I assume you—like the rest of your kind—have no financial sense.'

'Do you have to be so insulting?'

'Only to save you from yourself.' He leapt to his feet, took her in his arms and kissed her neck.

'What I need is someone to save me from you,' she said, squirming in his embrace, feeling her strength failing as his lips moved slowly along her chin to her mouth.

He hadn't kissed her since that first time. They hadn't mentioned it, but the sexual tension between them was hard to ignore. It made her angry. Why did it have to come to this? Why couldn't they just have a calm, friendly relationship? She wasn't ready for anything else.

The change she'd noticed in him was becoming more pronounced all the time. He was smiling more, was less serious and she knew it had to do with her. The implications did nothing to set her mind at ease. There was little she wanted less now than the amorous attentions of another man.

'Please Justin, don't,' she said forcefully. 'I mean it!' She pushed against him and eventually he released her. He shoved his hands into his pockets as if he were afraid he wouldn't be able to keep them off her. He looked at her for a long time without speaking. They stood facing each other in the small room, the air heavy with their feelings.

His eyes were very dark. His hair had fallen forward over his forehead and his mouth looked grim.

'Do you still love him?'

'I don't know,' she said tonelessly.

'The bastard *hit* you, and you *don't know*?'

She closed her eyes briefly. 'Please, Justin . . .'

His anger palpitated in the air. 'What did you feel when he hit you? What did you say?'

'I didn't say anything. He was gone before I realised what had happened.'

'How did you feel?'

She looked away. 'I felt degraded, enraged.'

'But you don't know that you don't love him anymore,' he said sarcastically.

She stiffened in anger. 'It's *not* that easy, Justin! Feelings aren't a maths problem! Add x and yes you love somebody or subtract y and you don't!' Her knees were shaking and she anchored her feet to the floor to steady herself.

'You've been here almost two months,' he said quietly. 'Why don't you relax and see what happens between us?'

'Justin, I *know* what will happen between us. I'm not stupid. Neither am I immune to your charms, but I don't think it's what I need right now.'

'You're fighting emotions with rational thought.'

'Yes, dammit! If I didn't do that, I'd have left weeks ago! I'd be back in Pennsylvania, thinking I should try again, because . . . because he needs me . . .' Her voice shook. 'You know how I feel? You want to know? I feel like I . . . I abandoned him! He was in trouble and I *left* him. If I loved him I should have stood by him no matter what.'

'There are limits to what any person can and should take, Linden, even in love. Getting beaten is not within those limits.'

'I *know* that, rationally. That's why I left.' Her legs had not stopped shaking and she stepped back and dropped into a chair. Leaning her head back she closed her eyes. 'When I think about it rationally I know there's nothing I can do for him any more. I tried everything. He wouldn't listen to me. He was too proud to admit he had a problem, too proud to find help. If I would have stayed with him he might have hurt me worse another time. If he hit me once he's likely to do it again. I keep saying that to myself over and over again. I keep telling myself I don't owe him anything. That I have too much self respect to ever accept that kind of treatment, that I think too much of myself to take the risk of his abuse again. Oh, God . . .' she moaned, hunching forward and pressing her fists against her eyes.

She felt his hands on her head and she didn't move. Then he took her wrists and pulled her fists away from her eyes.

He sat on his haunches in front of her, but his face was a blur as tears misted her eyes. She tried to smile, but her lips trembled. 'Oh, dear,' she said shakily, 'here I go again.' And she could feel the tears spill over and run down her cheeks.

'Come here,' he said softly, and pulled her gently out of the chair and on to his knees. They sat on the floor, she on his knees, curled together like lovers. And with her face pressed against his shoulder she cried for a long time and he never said a word.

They walked along the beach as the light was fading. The sun was low at the horizon and the shadows were long and distorted. Palms were dark silhouettes against the pearly colours of the sky.

She felt foolish, having given in to her misery with so much abandon, soaking his shirt with her tears. She took deep breaths of the clean salty air, swinging her arms to rid her body of tension.

'Let's go to the pier and watch the boats come in.' She looked at her watch. 'I guess they're in already, but we can watch them unload. I used to do that all the time when I came here as a girl. I'd bring my sketchbook and draw the boats and the fishermen hauling away the fish in the baskets on their shoulders.'

She'd tried twice again, bringing her easel and paints and positioning herself so she could see all that was going on. Twice she'd made a painting, with curious village children standing in a semi circle behind her, watching her paint. Both pictures had been gloomy and depressing. The sea had looked greyer than in reality, the men more tired, the boats more worn. It had not shown the laughter or the sunshine that was just as much a part of the scene. The piece of sandy beach had shown more garbage than there had been—more banana peels and coconut husks and broken beer bottles. These paintings were two of the ones hidden in the spare bedroom.

The pier jutted far out into the water, long and narrow and rickety, five planks wide attached to long vertical bamboo poles.

Four young fishermen in jeans and windbreakers sat on their haunches sorting out the pile of fish in their boat tied to the pier. They were talking and laughing as they worked, stopping for a moment to throw a curious look at Linden and Justin.

The next boat was already unloaded and on the deck lay a tangle of green fishing net, rope and brightly coloured floaters. A man was stirring a big steaming cooking pot on a kerosene burner that stood against the cabin wall. On a small piece of line above it hung several pieces of clothing. Linden wondered why he was cooking on his boat instead of eating at home in the village. Maybe he was single and lived on his boat and did not have a house.

At the far end of the pier they sat down, swinging their legs free over the water and looked out over the calm sea.

'Do you still think about her often? About Kate, I mean.' She didn't know what had made her ask the question.

'Now and then,' he said, not looking at her.

'Do you wish you had married her?'

He considered the question for a moment. 'There was a time that I did,' he said then. 'But not any more. I wasn't ready for marriage then, so it wouldn't have been right. But I do regret the way it ended. I regret having treated her the way I did—taking her for granted, not really listening to her. I was very selfish and inconsiderate.'

'Have you seen her at all since she left you?'

He shook his head. 'No. I did hear she married a year and a half later.'

They were silent for a while. Finally he turned to her, giving a funny little smile.

'It was all a long time ago.'

'Yes.'

There was another silence. She watched him as he gazed out over the ocean. He looked calm and relaxed. She liked his profile—a prominent nose, a strong chin. There was determination and strength in that face. He had spoken freely of his weaknesses, admitted them without making excuses. She liked that.

Her thoughts began to drift. She thought about painting the sunset, deciding against it. It was tacky and unoriginal and had been done a thousand times too often. She thought about Marinozzi who'd bought her painting.

'What do you know about this Marinozzi?' she asked. 'Is he Italian?'

'With that name and that accent I suppose he is, but he lives in Australia. At least that's the address he gave me.'

'I went to his house earlier today to tell him the painting was finished. He made a pass at me. Couldn't keep his hands to himself.'

'Can't blame the man,' he said levelly. 'Nothing ventured, nothing gained.'

'You're as disgusting as he is.'

'No I'm not,' he said, unperturbed. 'It took me weeks before I even *tried* to kiss you.'

'So what is wrong with you? Are you slow or something?'

He laughed out loud. 'First you say I'm disgusting for going after you, then you accuse me of being slow about it. Is that lack of logic the artist or the woman in you?'

'It must be my creative mind.'

'I thought so.'

Linden sighed. 'I'm hungry. I have this sudden mad craving for cheese. A piece of nice cheddar.'

'I'm afraid you won't find that here.'

'I know. Isn't it awful though that with all this delicious food here I still want something else?'

'Human nature. We always want what we can't have. I used to long for strawberries and cream.'

Linden looked pained. 'I don't want to hear about it.'

'I think Christmas on Penang will do us good. The hotels serve a traditional dinner for the tourists— turkey, the works.'

'I'm getting hungrier and hungrier.'

'All right. Come home with me and let's see what Ramaya has concocted.' He paused significantly. 'Unless of course you don't want to take the risk of my losing control over my passions and going for your body.'

'If you try, you'll be sorry,' she said, slicing the air with mock karate chops.

He laughed as he jumped to his feet. He held out his hand to help her up and she took it, smiling back at him.

CHAPTER FOUR

LINDEN awoke in the middle of the night to the sound of wind and rain, and she knew it was more than just another tropical rain storm. The wind howled like a living creature, shaking the house on its stilts and penetrating the walls. The wood moaned and groaned under the onslaught and the window shutters rattled even though they were closed and locked. She lay in bed, listening, feeling a growing sense of alarm. This was bad, worse than she'd ever experienced.

The air was filled with furious noise—the frantic swishing of the palms, the angry roaring of the ocean, the rain pounding on the ground and on the roof. The clamour was frightening and she had a sudden vision of the small island being torn loose by the force of the storm and floating and bobbing like a rudderless *sampan* on the seething ocean.

She looked at her watch. It was just after two in the morning, hours still until the first light would colour the sky and chase the night. She groped for the candle and the matches next to her bed. It took a lot of fumbling in the dark before she managed to light the candle and she was ridiculously grateful for the light. She slid out of bed and went over to the window. Carefully she opened the shutter a crack and peered outside. Wind and rain forced their way in and water dripped off her face. All she saw was an ominous wet blackness—no light anywhere, no moon in sight. Shivering, she closed the shutter. She looked around the bare room. What now? Sleep was out of the question. Maybe a cup of tea would settle her down. It would at least give her something to do.

Picking up the candle she made her way to the

kitchen. Her foot hit something wet and she slipped. Crying out, she grabbed the counter to steady herself, scraping her leg on a drawer handle. The candle fell to the floor and extinguished itself, leaving her in the blackest darkness she'd ever seen.

A cold drop fell on her bare shoulder, then another. A leak. The roof had not leaked before, but in this weather it was no surprise.

Carefully she lowered herself to the floor and, on hands and knees, searched for the fallen candle. It took her several endless minutes before she discovered it under a chair. She found the matches next to the gas ring and lit the candle again, breathing a sigh of relief.

There was a small puddle of water near the door. Looking up at the ceiling, she tried to locate the leak, but the candle was throwing wild dancing shadows all over the walls and she couldn't make out anything.

She found an enamel dishpan and put it under the drip. The water splattered loudly on the bottom—split splat split splat. Well, what was a little more noise? She ladled water into the kettle, lit the gas, and settled down on a stool to wait for it to boil. It seemed to take forever. Maybe she should light one of the kerosene lamps. Carrying the candle she cautiously made her way to the living room and brought one of the lamps back to the kitchen.

With a little more light, the world seemed not quite so hostile, although the howling wind and the roaring ocean outside made her feel anything but relaxed. Was Justin up too? Or was he asleep and oblivious to the hellish spectacle outside? He was so close, yet so far. A frightening sense of isolation began to take hold of her.

The water boiled and she made a pot of tea. First she carried the candle and a cup to the bedroom, then went back for the lamp and the teapot, walking slowly, looking for signs of other leaks.

Wrapped up in a sheet, she huddled in bed, holding the cup of steaming flower tea in both hands. The din outside had not diminished. Somewhere she heard the metallic screeching of tearing metal. Maybe the corrugated iron roof of one of the houses had fallen victim to the wind. She visualised water pouring into the house. She thought of terrified children, crying babies, desperate parents. She tried to banish the images from her mind. The storm raged on. Now and then a coconut crashed to the ground and all around in the night were other noises, unidentifiable, frightening. The rain kept coming down on in a relentless downpour. The village would be flooded, crops drowned in water and beaten down by the force of wind and rain. Tomorrow when it had all finished, the spectacle would be one of devastation. *I hope nobody dies* she kept thinking.

She willed the morning to come, but time crept by torturously slowly, as she drank one cup of tea after another until finally the pot was empty. She picked up the book she'd been reading before going to sleep and tried to read, but it was useless. There was no way her mind could be diverted with the racket going on outside. Closing her eyes she lay back on her pillow and rolled up into a ball under the sheet. Several minutes later she tore the pillow from under her head and covered her face with it, but even then the noise was still there.

For a few moments she considered leaving the house and going over to Justin's. Could she possibly make it? The wind might sweep her away and smash her against a house or a tree, or wash her out to sea. It would be madness, sheer madness.

A deafening noise of something crashing suddenly filled the air. The house shook violently. Her body froze and her heart stopped for a terrifying instant. The sound of tearing metal and splintering wood screeched through the air. Her heart began to pound in heavy, painful thuds and clutching the sheet, she looked in terror at the ceiling and walls. The house was coming down. It had to be coming down. She couldn't move, sat staring at the walls in frozen panic as the noise suddenly ceased.

It was over. She jumped out of bed, looking around wildly. I've got to get out of here, she thought. *I've got to get out of here!* Her legs were shaking violently with the shock. With trembling hands she tied a sarong around her, took the lamp and carefully opened the bedroom door. Everything looked as it had before, except the front door which was banging in the wind. She looked out into the night. There were no stairs. The overhang, corrugated iron with thatch, was gone.

The wind whipped the hair around her head and the rain had soaked her the minute she'd looked outside. *I can't get out!* The thought filled her with panic. Down below was a swirling mass of mud and what she assumed was the debris of the broken steps and overhang—a heap of splintered wood and twisted metal. She'd break or lacerate something jumping into the rubble.

Then she noticed the light. At the same time, above the howling of the wind, she heard her name called. An indescribable sense of relief flooded her.

'Justin! I'm here!' she called at the top of her voice.

The light came closer. 'Are you all right?' he shouted.

'Yes!' Could he hear her? The wind seemed to sweep her words away, cutting off her breath. 'I'm all right,' she called again. 'But I can't get out!' She was still holding the lamp, hanging on to the doorpost with her other hand.

He was close now, slowly picking his way through the rubble, fighting wind and rain. Then he was directly underneath her, moving aside wood and metal. It seemed to take forever. By the light of his flashlight she could see the remains of the steps and overhang, and a coconut palm sprawling on top of it.

'Listen to me!' he shouted. 'Blow out the lamp!

Turn around and hang off the edge of the floor! Can you hear me?'

'I can hear you!'

'When you're hanging all the way down, let go. I'm right here. I'll catch you.'

She blew out the lamp and put it inside. He shone his flashlight at the edge of the floor. She tested it with her foot. It seemed solid enough. She went down on her haunches and ran her hand along the edge to check for nails or sharp splinters. It seemed all right. She turned around and went down on her knees. Carefully she lowered her legs over the edge and leaned on her stomach. The wind lashed at her soaked sarong and the rain pounded down on her back. Then slowly she slid the rest of her body downward over the edge until she hung only by her hands. Her muscles cramped in fear and she had a brief vision of broken arms and legs.

'Let go!' he shouted.

Closing her eyes, she released her hands from their grip. She felt his hands slide over her thighs and hips, then they clamped around her waist in an iron grip. The next instant they were both falling, landing in the mud with her sprawling on her back across his chest.

She felt nothing. Then his hands moved her again, turning her over until she lay with her face on his wet chest and the rest of her dragging in the mire. She went limp. She couldn't feel, she couldn't think.

'I'm sorry,' he said in her ear. 'I slipped and lost my balance. Are you hurt?'

'No, no.' She felt the drumming of his heart against her cheek. She lifted her head, but it was too dark to see anything but the contours of his face. She pushed herself to her knees, realising the sarong had come undone and was twisted half around her ankles, half dragging in the muck. Justin came to his feet too and reached for the flashlight which he'd positioned on a piece of the ravished steps and directed at the doorway. He turned it on her and gave a roar of laughter.

'Please!' she yelled furiously. 'Do me a favour!' She grabbed the sarong out of the mud, but he took the sodden thing from her fingers and threw it down again.

'Leave it!' He took her hand and pulled her away, shining the flashlight on the ground in front of them. 'Be careful!' He put his arm around her shoulders to steady her.

It took all her strength to stay on her feet as they slipped and slithered through mud and water with the wind tearing at them with unbelievable force.

How they finally made it the short distance to Justin's house, she had no idea. Somehow she must have climbed the stairs, somehow she must have entered the house.

He pushed her into the bathroom. Her teeth were chattering and she leaned against the wall with her eyes closed.

When she opened them again, Justin had lit a lamp and put it down on a stool. She looked at him, not believing what she saw. He was covered in mud from top to toe, one solid mass of wet brown. She looked down at herself. She was stark naked, but covered with muck it didn't make much difference. She began to laugh. First softly, then harder and she couldn't help herself. Her knees gave way and her back slid down along the tile until she was kneeling on the floor, still laughing.

She saw Justin's face break into a grin and then he was laughing too. Tears were running down her cheeks and the relief it brought was wonderful. Tension ebbed away and when the laughter finally subsided, she felt almost normal again.

Only her legs were far from steady when she tried to stand up and she was still shivering from cold.

'Grit your teeth,' he said. 'I'll rinse you off, but the

water is cold.' He lowered the blue dipper in the bucket of water and poured it over her head. The breath caught in her throat, then she shrieked.

'Stop it! I can do it myself!'

'Like hell you can! You can hardly stand on your legs!' This was followed with another dipper of water and she gritted her teeth when the cold hit her. Then he threw some water over himself and washed his face.

'All right,' he said then, 'let's get serious about this.' He picked up a bar of soap and made an attempt to wash her.

She struck at his hands. 'You lecher! Give it to me!'

Grinning he handed it over and she turned her back on him and she quickly soaped herself all over. 'Some more water, please.'

He poured more water over her, but the mud streaming down her body never seemed to end. Her hair was full of it and it took forever to get it all out. She was exhausted, standing there struggling with the mass of wet hair in the middle of the night, shivering and shaking. She was uneasy and uncomfortable with him standing right behind her, but there was little choice but to bear it. He wouldn't leave her and she hadn't the strength for a futile argument about it.

He gave her a huge bath towel to wrap herself up in and he watched her until she was safely sitting on the couch.

'Just give me a few minutes and I'll get myself clean,' he said. 'Then we'll have something to drink. Just don't move!'

Twenty minutes later, with a shot of whisky in her belly, she began to feel warmer. 'Do you have another towel,' she asked. 'My hair is dripping.'

He got one for her and she let him squeeze out the water from her hair. 'Would you like me to brush it out?' he asked. 'If you don't mind using my brush.'

She hesitated. If she didn't brush it out now, she

would pay for it dearly tomorrow. 'It should be brushed,' she said, 'but I can do it myself.'

'I don't doubt it for a moment,' he answered drily, leaving the room to find the brush. 'Sit up straight and lean your head on the back of the chair,' he ordered when he returned.

She did as she was told, drowsy with the whisky and tired. She closed her eyes. It was a wonderful sensuous feeling to have someone do your hair. Some leftover primitive grooming instinct from the darkness of the human past. It amazed her how gentle Justin was, not tearing at her hair to straighten out the tangles. It took quite a while before the brush ran smoothly through the whole length of hair, and by then she was half asleep.

'Thank you,' she murmured. It was an effort to open her eyes. He was standing in front of her, looking down at her.

'It's still wet.'

She nodded. 'Doesn't matter.' Her eyes drooped again. She felt herself being lifted out of the chair and she opened her eyes again, seeing the left side of his face.

'Justin, what . . .?'

'Put your arms around my neck,' he ordered. 'I'm not Samson and I might drop you if you don't hold on.'

Again she did as she was told. It was a good, safe feeling to be held so close and she leaned her face against his shoulder. He took her out of the room and a moment later she was deposited on a bed, and she had to let go of him.

She heaved a deep sigh and went limp again as she felt the comfort of the mattress.

He sat down on the edge of the bed and leaned over her. She smiled at him and closed her eyes again. It seemed impossible to keep them open.

'Listen!' he said softly.

She listened. Something was different. The howling had stopped. 'The wind is going down,' she whispered.

'The rain too.'

'Yes.' It was still coming down heavily, but nothing compared to the ferocious torrents of a while ago. 'I'm glad,' she murmured. 'Let's just hope some of my house is still standing.'

'I think it's just the steps and the overhang. We'll see in the morning when it gets light.'

'I'm so tired,' she whispered.

'I can tell.'

'I woke up at two. The noise was so bad, I couldn't sleep.'

'Now you can.' She felt his mouth on hers, a gentle touching that stirred something deep inside her. She put her arms around his neck and his kiss grew more intimate. A soft moan escaped her as she responded to it. It felt good, so good, with the warmth sparking into excitement and deeply buried longings surfacing. She clung to him as he released her.

'Don't go,' she whispered.

'Go to sleep, Linden.' His voice sounded rough, but it didn't really register. Thoughts faded as she drifted away into the soft darkness of sleep.

Coming back to consciousness seemed to take a long time. She floated back and forth between half-sleep and semi-wakefulness, never quite waking fully. For short moments she would look around the room in the dim grey light, not recognising it, then drifting off again.

She surfaced, finally, remembering where she was and why.

It was still raining, a soft, steady splashing on the greenery outside. The light was grey and dull.

The bed was much like her own with a kapok mattress. She was covered with a sheet and a light blanket and the towel she'd been wearing lay bunched up at her feet.

Sliding her legs over the side of the bed, she sat up and pushed the hair out of her face and over her shoulders. Her body felt heavy and sluggish and she came to her feet slowly. Ouch! She lifted her feet to look at them. Last night she'd been barefoot and there were scratches on the soles.

A sarong hung over a chair and she wrapped it around her and opened the door.

The house was silent. Where was Justin? On bare feet she walked around the empty rooms. No Justin. No Ramaya, either. There were signs of breakfast in the kitchen—an empty coffee cup, a frying pan on the stove, a plate with bread crumbs and congealing egg yolk.

Where had Justin slept last night? It could only have been the couch for there were no other beds in the house. She grinned. What a gentleman, letting her take over his bed.

A grey-green, dripping world greeted her as she opened the front door. She shivered. It was almost cold. Noises came from the direction of her house and she peered through the curtain of drizzling rain to see. A shape was moving around, lifting and pulling metal. It must be Justin, examining the damage. She'd need something on her feet if she was going over there to have a look. In the bedroom she found a pair of Justin's thongs and slipped them on. They were miles too big and looked ridiculous. Well, no matter. She flip-flopped carefully through the house and down the stairs, feeling the rain cold on her skin.

Last night in the dark she had not been able to see what exactly had happened. In the light of morning it was quite clear. A coconut palm had been uprooted, had crashed down on the overhang and the steps and torn it all down. The roof had been spared, as had the main part of the house. It really wasn't all that bad.

Last night in that terrible deluge it had seemed as if the house had been coming down around her.

'What are you doing?' she asked, and he turned, surprised.

'Well, hello there. I didn't see you coming.'

'Hi. Boy what a mess!'

'It's not so bad. You're lucky. From what I hear some people lost their entire roof, not to speak of all the damage to the crops.'

She nodded. 'I won't complain. Did anybody get hurt?'

He shook his head. 'Not seriously. Just minor scrapes and bruises.'

Linden surveyed the mangled steps and overhang. 'Do you know someone who can fix this?'

He rubbed his muddy hands on the side of his jeans. 'Not immediately. I checked. Everybody is busy right now. The roofs obviously have priority. But we can get you a bamboo ladder so you can at least get in and out of the place.' He surveyed the rubble around him. 'First we'd better get that palm out of the way. I'll get an axe and chop it into manageable pieces.'

She frowned. 'Are you sure we can't find someone to do that? You have work to do. I don't like to take your time.'

He shrugged. 'It'll be a lot faster if I just do it. Besides, some hard physical work will do me good.' He grinned and flexed the muscles of his back and shoulders. 'It might help me get rid of all the knots from sleeping on the damn couch. The thing is only about three feet too short.'

She looked pained. 'I'm sorry, I'm sorry. Please don't give me a guilt complex.'

'All right. Make me another cup of coffee and we'll be even. Dry yourself off first. There's another sarong in the closet in my bedroom. Second shelf from the top. I'll be up in ten minutes.'

She flip-flopped back through the mud, the soaked

sarong clinging to her. She'd pay a small fortune to be able to get into her house and get some decent clothes, or at least a bra and a shirt. She must look a sight.

The mirror in the bathroom confirmed her suspicions. Her hair had dried while she slept and looked wild and unkempt, sticking out in weird waves and peaks. And now it was wet again from the rain. I look like a madwoman, she thought, and couldn't control a chuckle. If that didn't turn Justin off romantically, nothing would.

With Justin's brush she tried to make some order out of her unruly mane, but it was a hopeless endeavour. There had to be a rubber band somewhere, so she could at least tie it back. But short of digging through his every drawer, she didn't find one any place. In the kitchen she discovered a piece of pink raffia packing string. She tried to tie it around her hair, but it wouldn't get a good grip and kept sliding down as soon as she moved. Well, it had to do for the moment.

She felt like an intruder looking in Justin's closet for a sarong. Not that there was anything exciting to be seen there, but it seemed such an indiscreet thing to do, even on invitation. Several sarongs were right there next to a stack of coloured undershorts. On a shelf below were some tee-shirts. Hesitating only for a moment, she picked up the one from the top and looked at it. It was much too big for her, but at least she wouldn't feel so naked. She pulled it over her head, tied the sarong around her waist, pushed up the string in her hair, and set off for the kitchen.

A few minutes later Justin came in, dripping wet, and sat down at the small kitchen table which she'd just cleared of his breakfast dishes.

'I've got the axe,' he announced, drying his hair with a towel Linden handed him.

She placed the coffee in front of him. 'Can I do something?'

He shook his head. 'It's not much of a job. I'm just going to chop the thing in a few pieces so I can move it out of the way. It shouldn't take very long.' He drank his coffee gratefully. 'What you can do, if you wouldn't mind, is fix us some lunch in an hour or so. Ramayah didn't show up this morning, so I expect she has problems of her own today.'

'In an hour? What time is it?'

He glanced at his watch. 'Eleven-thirty almost.'

'Good heavens, I just got up.'

'You did seem to be sleeping peacefully.'

'You checked up on me?'

'Just peeked in for a moment before I left.'

'Hadn't you seen enough?' she asked, mildly mocking.

He shook his head solemnly, but his eyes were laughing. 'It's never enough, don't you know that?'

She picked up the empty coffee cups and turned without answering.

'You have a beautiful body, Linden,' he said to her back.

'Shut up, Justin, I don't want to hear about it.'

'Very beautiful,' he persisted. 'I had a hard time keeping my hands off you last night.' A slight pause. 'You didn't seem to mind. Even asked me to stay.'

'You're a liar.'

'I'm not. Boy scout's honour.'

'I don't remember a thing.' She washed the coffee cups, gritting her teeth.

'Who's a liar, sweet Linden?'

The cup handle snapped off in her hand. 'Damn,' she muttered. 'I broke your cup. I'm sorry.'

He was standing behind her back and put his arms around her, taking the cup out of her hand. She stiffened in his embrace.

'Let go of me, Justin.'

'You liked it last night. You were all soft, sweet and willing.'

'I had a belly full of whisky, what did you expect?'

'Not a belly full. Only one meagre shot.'

'Well, whatever.' It was hard to try and not move, to try and not feel anything.

He kissed her neck. 'If one shot of whisky is all it takes, we could try again tonight.'

'You can forget it. The rain has stopped, by the way. Why don't you take your axe and work out your frustrations on the coconut palm?'

He straightened and released her. 'You really know how to make a guy feel good,' he said sarcastically, and strode out of the kitchen.

'I try,' she said, smiling sweetly at his retreating back.

Linden positioned herself in front of the small Chinese temple and examined the subject. The temple was on the other side of the village, and she'd hired Faisal and his bicycle to transport her easel, stool and paints. She'd watched him fearfully as he'd taken off with easel balancing precariously on a small platform attached to the back of the bike, wondering if the thing would fall off and break in half. It wasn't collapsible, which didn't make it an easy object for moving around.

She'd been feeling better lately, less depressed. Maybe purging her misery out on poor Justin's shirt front a few days ago had helped, she didn't know. But painting the small temple seemed a good thing to do. It certainly was cheerful enough with its red and gold paint and colourful carved dragons that sat patiently on the roof waiting for who knows what.

The sun was white and blinding, the sky an endless, brilliant blue. Not a cloud to be seen anywhere. It was incredible that only yesterday morning she'd woken to the ravishes of the worst storm she'd ever seen. That same afternoon she was back in her house, climbing a rickety bamboo ladder Justin had found for her. Everything had been the way she had left it the night before. The kitchen floor was wet, but had been quickly dried. A carpenter would come tomorrow morning to build new steps and replace the overhang. At least she had enough money to pay for the repairs from the sale of her painting to the miserable Marinozzi.

With some quick strokes she drew the outline of the temple on the canvas. It would be a challenge this, but she felt up to it today. She worked with concentration for a long time, trying to ignore the curious onlookers who came by now and then. The faint smell of incense was in the air, even here, out in the open. Through the open temple doors she could see the glimmer of the huge brass pot that held the smoking joss sticks.

When she got tired, she stopped for a while, sitting down in the grass in the shade of a clove tree. She'd brought coffee in a thermos and she sipped it slowly, looking around. From where she sat now, the angle was different, and with a sudden leap of excitement she noticed the simple little church spire with its cross on top poking up into the sky behind the ornately carved dragons on the temple roof.

'Perfect!' she said out loud. She jumped up, almost spilling the coffee, and rushed back to her easel. From here she couldn't see the church spire. If she moved in order to get the church into view, the temple would be seen from a different angle. For an artist no problem. She moved the easel, painted in the spire, leaving the temple the way it was. After all this was not a photograph. Stepping back, she examined her work, chewing at the end of her brush. It was good! It still needed a lot of work, but she was getting there. She was filled with elation. She wanted to go home and show Justin. Now, before it was even finished.

As she stood there, scrutinising the painting, a momentous realisation came to her. *I want to show it to Justin,* she'd thought. Not *I wish Waite could see this.*'

For a moment she was overwhelmed by a strange mingling of emotions—an utter sense of relief and a deep sorrow.

CHAPTER FIVE

JUSTIN was not at home. She couldn't believe it. He was always home around this time. It was only half-past twelve. Normally he was at his typewriter until one, then had lunch. She felt a deep disappointment, out of all proportion, she knew.

'Where did he go,' she asked Ramayah, and the woman shrugged.

'He went out in his boat.'

Out in his boat. 'When will he come back?'

'Later this afternoon.'

Linden turned dejectedly and went home. Maybe he had writer's block and had decided to clear his head out on the open water. Maybe he'd gone to Penang—not that that would make much sense. They were going there for Christmas in three days. She stood on her verandah and peered out over the sea. At the horizon there were a few boats, but they were all fishing trawlers. There wasn't a small motor-boat in sight.

Shrugging, she went inside and had her lunch. Nazirah had made her *laksa*, a sourish fish soup with rice noodles and vegetables, one of her specialities. She had sprinkled on the top slices of an edible pink flower that made the dish look beautiful and elegant.

After lunch Linden washed her hair, rinsing out the last of the mud, wrote a letter to Liz and another to her sister. Then she picked up a Wilbur Smith novel, soon losing herself in the story of pioneer life in South Africa—gold mining, elephant hunting, family life in the empty bush.

A loud knocking jerked her back to the present and she jumped up to see who was there. The door was open to facilitate the movement of air through the house and Mr Marinozzi stood in the doorway with a sickly sweet smile on his unshaven face.

'Good afternoon.'

She did not smile back. 'Good afternoon. What can I do for you?'

His eyes slid over her body and a cold shiver ran down her spine. She tossed her still-damp hair back over her shoulders and gave him a stony look. He kept smiling, unperturbed and gestured at the temple painting in the middle of the room. 'I see you are working on another masterpiece.'

She nodded without replying.

'Do you have any others I could see?'

'I'm sorry, no.' She wasn't going to show him the ones she wasn't happy with. She didn't really want the man in the house at all.

'None at all?'

She shook her head. 'No.'

'What about this one? How long will it take to finish?'

With a certainty beyond any doubt, she knew she didn't want him to have the painting, not this one. 'It's not for sale.'

'Surely for the right price. . . .'

'Not for any price, Mr Marinozzi.'

'Well, think about it. Do you mind if I have a look at it when it's finished?'

'Not in the least, but don't count on my changing my mind, Mr Marinozzi. I won't.'

'We'll see.' He smiled indulgingly and she felt like slapping his flabby, stubbly face. He was a man who was used to getting what he wanted, she was quite sure. All he had to do was open his wallet. Well, he wasn't buying her painting.

He left then, much to her relief. She went back to the verandah and brushed her hair. She heard someone whistling and looking up she saw Justin coming down the path towards her house, a package in his hand.

'Come on up!' she called right before he rounded the house and disappeared out of sight. A moment later she heard his steps on the creaky floor boards of the living room, then they stopped. He was looking at the painting, she realised and came hastily up out of her chair and went inside.

He looked at her as she entered and by the expression on his face she could tell he liked what he saw.

'That's going to be one hell of a painting,' he said.

She felt immensely happy with his praise. Then she noticed the small frown and wondered what he was seeing.

'You know,' he said thoughtfully, 'I've walked by the temple a hundred times and I never noticed the church behind it.'

'It isn't.'

'It isn't?'

'Not if you look at it from the road. You know the clove tree on the right of the temple? I was sitting there when I noticed the church spire above the temple roof. But the angle for painting the temple from here was all wrong, so I took a few liberties, and voilà.'

He nodded. 'Artistic licence. Very well employed, I must say.'

She curtsied. 'Thank you kindly, sir.'

He looked down on the package in his hand as if he had forgotten he had it. 'For you,' he said, handing it to her.

'For me?' She took it, surprised. It was heavy and solid. She unwrapped the paper, curious. 'Cheese! Cheddar!' She looked at him, feeling more touched than she wanted to admit. 'Where did you get it?'

'Penang.'

So that's what he'd been doing today. Half an hour

to Telok Bahang. Forty-five minutes or so from the wharf to George Town, to a supermarket.

'You went all the way to George Town for a piece of cheese?' she asked incredulously, and he laughed at her expression.

'No. I went to Batu Feringghi, to the Hotel Rasa Sayang. Had some lunch in the coffee shop. When I was finished eating, this sweet young thing asked me if I wanted anything else. I said yes, one pound of cheddar cheese please. You should have seen her face.' He grinned at the memory.

'Did she give it to you?'

'Eventually. The manager is a friend of mine, so it wasn't any problem.'

'Thank you.' The cheese felt like a block of gold in her hand. 'That was very thoughtful of you.' She looked away, suddenly embarrassed by what she was feeling. 'Come, let's have some.'

They went into the kitchen, filled a woven bamboo tray with a knife, plates, sliced mango and papaya and some crisp shrimp crackers left over from lunch.

Linden examined the contents of the refrigerator. 'There's a ripe avocado. Shall I cut that up too?'

'Sure. I'll go home and get a bottle of wine. I'll be right back.'

He returned with a bottle of Bordeaux and a small cassette player.

'Where did you get the wine?' she asked. 'The Rasa Sayang?'

He laughed. 'No. Once in a while I go to George Town and do some shopping. This was left over from my last spree. I'm afraid I do not own any wine glasses, though.'

'Neither do I.' She placed two water glasses on the tray. 'These will do just fine. Even hold more.'

They carried the tray to the verandah and settled down to eat the feast. Justin switched on the cassette player and the mellow sounds of old jazz wafted into the air. He pulled out another cassette from his pocket. 'Beethoven, if you prefer.'

'I like jazz. This is wonderful.' She sighed with delighted contentment. 'Let's eat. I'm starving.' She tossed her hair back over her shoulder and took knife to cheese.

'I checked on our reservations for Christmas,' he commented after the first of their hunger was appeased. 'I sent a message last week, but since I was there I thought I might as well check out our rooms.'

'Where? At the Rasa Sayang? Justin, you can't do that! It'll cost a fortune!'

'I get a special discount. Besides, all my socks are getting full of royalty money I'm not spending. What am I going to do when I run out of socks?'

'You're crazy!'

'Don't look so worried. It's only two nights. It's hardly going to break me.'

'Justin, that's not the point! I can't accept it. I want to pay for my own room.' It had been wrong in the first place to accept his offer. She valued her independence. Always before she'd paid her own way, or her fair share. Having a job and a paycheque, there seemed to be no reason not to.

There was a silence as they looked at each other—a challenge of wills.

'All right,' Justin said at last. 'I'll make you a deal. I'll pay for our Christmas expenses and you give me one of your paintings in return.'

She thought about it for a moment. 'Do you actually *want* one of my paintings? You said yourself, the price of art is worth it only if you find it worth it.'

'Why are you so suspicious? I like what I've seen of your work, you know that. Especially the last two. I'd like very much to have one.'

'All right, then. It's a deal.'

He refilled their glasses with wine. 'I saw Mr

Marinozzi before I came here. He said he's buying your temple picture.'

Anger swelled inside her. 'I told him it wasn't for sale. I don't like the man. I don't want him to have it.'

'He seems to think he's getting it.'

'He seems to think if he offers me enough money I'll cave in. He said there's a price for everything.'

'There is.'

'Not for that painting! Not from him, anyway!' The plate slid off her lap and dropped on the floor, breaking in two. 'Oh damn,' she muttered, going down on her knees to pick up the pieces. He followed her into the kitchen where she dumped the broken plate into the garbage pail.

'Don't let him upset you. He's not worth it.'

'I'm not upset. I'm *mad*. How long is he staying here, anyway?'

'Two more weeks. You think you'll survive it?' He smiled good-humouredly.

She sighed, then laughed. 'Oh, I guess so. Shall I make some coffee?'

She was still a little fuzzy-headed from the wine when he stood up to leave an hour later. It was dark in the house, but she hadn't yet lit the lamps.

'Thanks again for the cheese,' she said. 'That was one of the nicest presents I've ever had.'

She thought of the many presents Waite had given her over the past two years. Every time he'd had one of his foul moods he came, penitent, with something else. Large bunches of red roses. Gold earrings. Huge boxes of imported chocolates. Silk scarves. Crystal wine glasses. Until in the end she'd wanted to throw them back into his face. The presents were given to appease his own guilt, a plea to her not to stop loving him.

Justin had given her the cheese to please *her*. Not out of guilt, not to impress her with his generosity or his money. Just to please her.

He stood close to her near the door and the look in his eyes made her heart flutter uneasily. His hands reached out and slid down the length of her hair.

'You have beautiful hair,' he said softly. 'I like it when it's loose like this.' He took a handful and tugged at it gently and she moved a little closer, keeping her eyes trained on the buttons of his shirt, pale glimmers in the dark. He let her hair slide through his fingers, putting his hands on both sides of her face, lifting it to his.

She stood very still, her heart throbbing, and she looked into his eyes and she knew she wanted him to kiss her. But he did not move, just looked at her, caressing her with his eyes. The hands at the side of her face were cool against her warm skin. She ached to touch him too—feel his hair and his face and the strong muscles of his back. Slowly she lifted her arms, sliding them around his back and flattened her hands against it.

His breathing was as shallow as hers. She noticed it with a strange excitement. 'Justin,' she whispered, 'please kiss me.'

He bent his head to hers and she closed her eyes and for an agonising moment she felt nothing. Then his mouth covered hers and fire leaped up inside her, spreading hot through her limbs. His hands slid down from her face, down her arms and sides and around her back. She moved her own around his neck and they clung together as they kissed.

Her head swam. He was holding her so tightly she couldn't breathe. She broke away, gasping, stunned by the sudden unleashing of passion. He stepped back, raking his hand through his hair, breathing hard. They stared at each other in the darkness, seeing only shapes and shadows, feeling the electric heat surrounding them.

She couldn't think of what to say. Her knees were

shaking and with her hands she searched for the wall behind her and leaned against it.

'I think I'd better go,' he said at last, opening the door. With one foot on the top step of the stairs, he looked back at her.

She swallowed hard. 'Go, Justin. Please, go.'

The next morning Linden went back to the temple and worked on the painting, applying herself with so much concentration that there was no thought of anything else.

The dragons were giving her trouble, as were the intricate black Chinese characters on the big gold sign above the door. Although generally she didn't copy photographically, it seemed important that at least the characters should have some authenticity. Also, if she didn't get the strokes right, who knows what blasphemous meaning they could take on. The smaller characters along the door frame caused no problem. Just some faint gold smudges would do. Nobody would be able to read anything in them, at least she hoped not. Better check it out with a friendly soul, she decided.

When Faisal and his bicycle came again to help her with the transport of her equipment, she asked him to stop at Mak Long Teh's cart. She was busy serving a customer, a skinny old man in shirt and sarong. When he had finished eating his *mee* and had returned his bowl, Linden took the painting off the bike and showed it to the woman.

'What do you think, Mak Long Teh?'

A look of surprise passed over the woman's face. 'You are a painter?'

Linden nodded. 'Do you like it?'

Mak Long Teh scrutinised the picture. 'It's very beautiful.' Then she shook her head and pointed at the church spire. 'I don't think the church is there.'

'I know. I thought it looked nice. What about the Chinese words? Did I paint them right?'

Mak Long Teh laughed. 'A little bit.'

'It doesn't say something bad?'

The woman shook her head. 'No, no, it's beautiful.'

'But a little bit funny?' She had the horrible suspicion she wasn't getting a straight answer. It wouldn't be good manners to say something negative.

'No, no, it's beautiful.'

They were surrounded by people, young ones and old ones, all looking and pointing at the picture. An old man's spindly finger almost touched the canvas, pointing at the church spire. 'It isn't there,' he said in Malay.

'I know, I know.' Why were they all so interested in the church spire? She wanted to know about the Chinese characters. She glanced around the circle of on-lookers, searching for Chinese faces. There were a number of them. She pointed at the black characters.

'I am a dumb foreigner,' she said in English, repeating it in her best Malay. The crowd burst out laughing. 'I don't know Chinese writing,' she continued. 'You tell me, is this bad?' They all laughed again. She wasn't sure what the joke was, but they certainly thought it was funny.

I'm a stand-up comic, she thought. I might as well give up. The Malay don't know Chinese characters and the Chinese aren't telling.

'It is not bad!' said Mak Long Teh next to her. 'It is beautiful!'

Justin stood in her living room, looking at the painting. She hadn't seen him in two days and she felt a slight unease. Trying to shrug it off, she moved next to him and pointed at the sign above the temple entrance.

'I'm having trouble with the Chinese characters.'

'They look fine to me.'

'You're not Chinese.'

He glanced at her. 'You have a point there.'

She told him what had happened when she'd shown Mak Long Teh the painting. 'I suppose I should have known I wasn't going to get a straight answer.' She shrugged. 'I'll just have to hope for the best.'

'Don't worry about it. I was thinking, how about painting in the mosque minarette on the other side?' His eyes were laughing at her.

'Good idea. And while I'm at it, maybe a Hindu temple as well.'

'Well, why not?'

'You have no artistic sense, do you?' she asked. 'Overkill won't do. I think I'll just keep it simple.' She smiled. 'Besides, the people would have a fit. They were already wondering what the church spire was doing there.'

A bicycle bell rang outside.

'Here's Faisal with my curry buns. How about some coffee or tea?'

'Coffee, thanks.'

Fast feet stomped on the wooden stairs and Faisal appeared in the open door with a paper package in his hand. His black hair was ruffled from riding the bike. He wore shorts and a shirt and thongs on his feet. He was a handsome boy with dark intelligent eyes. He thanked her politely when she paid him, then rushed down the stairs in a hurry for his next errand.

'He's quite an entrepreneur, that kid. He helps me carry my easel and stool around sometimes.'

'Shouldn't he be in school?'

'I asked him. He said it was not necessary. He doesn't like school. He wants to make money and get rich.'

'Did you inform him of the fact that in order to get rich you need to make *a lot* of money, and that to make a lot of money it helps to be educated?'

'I most certainly did! He said he knows how to read and write and he knows his maths, and as far as he is concerned that's all that's necessary.' She paused, frowning. 'And what is this? Are you accusing me? He's not out of school because of me, you know. I saw him riding around on his bike for weeks before I even asked him.'

'I'm not accusing you of anything. I'm just wondering why the kid isn't in school when the law says he should be.'

'Well, ask the law, not me.' She marched off to the kitchen in righteous indignation.

'Hey!' he called out, following her. 'You wanna pick a fight?'

She looked at him wide-eyed. 'Pick a fight? Me? I never pick a fight.' From the big container on the counter she ladled water into the kettle and put it on the gas ring.

'No,' he said blandly, 'you're not the type. Even-tempered, easy-going . . .'

'Right. Hand me the sugar bowl, will you?'

He gave it to her. 'About tomorrow. I want to leave early. Go to George Town to spend the day and come back to the hotel in the evening. How does that suit you?'

'I'd like that.'

'By the way,' he said carefully, as they sat on the verandah drinking their coffee. 'I have another letter for you.' He took it from his pocket and tossed it on the table.

Linden put the curry bun down. Her heart was beating nervously as she picked the envelope up. It was Liz's neat round handwriting. She put it back down.

'Thanks. I wonder why they can't deliver it here. This is the third time they've given my mail to you.'

'Life is full of mysteries. Especially in the Far East.'

'Yeah, tell me about it.'

He stood up to go a short time later. He bent over her, kissed her quickly on the mouth, then straightened up again. 'Don't let that letter upset you. And if it does, I live right over there.' He thumbed at his house, then turned and was off.

She ripped open the envelope. There was a Christmas card inside—a snowy winter scene with children skating on a frozen pond surrounded by naked trees whose branches stuck up dark and stark against the grey sky.

There was no news at all, Liz wrote. It was freezing cold and she still had no man to warm her bed. 'Where are they all?' she asked. 'I am not ugly, poor, dumb, or neurotic (well, maybe a little, but aren't we all?). All I want is a man who is also not ugly, poor, dumb or neurotic (at least not too much).' She was so desperate, she wrote, that she'd accepted an invitation from a co-worker who sported day-glo ties and a Watusi hair-do.

It was with some relief that Linden noticed that Liz did not mention Waite. Maybe he had given up visiting her to squeeze her for information.

She went into the village to buy some toothpaste and had her dinner in a small restaurant, sitting outside at a wobbly table on a collapsible metal chair. A Chinese woman in green flowered polyester pyjamas and wooden sandals took her order of fried rice and chicken *satay*. Her sandals went clip-clop on the stones as she retreated to the kitchen.

An Indian girl brought her the food. She was very dark with long black hair in a braid down her back, just like her own. The girl wore a sarong and a tunic with long sleeves.

Linden slid the *satay* from the wooden skewers with her fork. The plate had a border of pink roses and was heaped high with rice. A lot of food for very little money, more than she could possibly eat. She looked around as she ate, taking in the busy street scene. It was dark and kerosene lamps burned everywhere. Shops were open doing business. People were laughing and talking, and children were still playing in the streets. Somewhere a radio played loudly, emitting Malay pop songs.

'Good evening.'

Julio Marinozzi. All dressed up in Givenchy shirt and expensive-looking pants that nonetheless did not hide his pot belly. She looked at the man with dread. Oh, no, she thought. I don't need him now. He ruins my appetite.

'Good evening,' she said coolly.

'Eating alone?'

'Yes.'

'Do you mind if I join you?'

Yes, I do, she thought, but good manners got the best of her. 'Please do.' She hoped he'd fall through the chair. Which, of course, he didn't.

'I stopped by your house,' he said, 'but you were not there. But I had not expected to find you here.'

'Why not?' She took a forkful of rice and brought it to her mouth.

'A lady alone at night?' he asked silkily.

It took a moment to chew and swallow her food.

'It's only seven o'clock. And this isn't Rome. Or Sydney, or New York, for that matter. I'm perfectly safe here.' As long you and your sickening smile stay away from me, she added silently.

The woman in the pyjama outfit clip-clopped to the table. Julio Marinozzi ordered a cup of tea. When the Indian girl brought it to the table he gave her a lascivious look and Linden nearly kicked him under the table. Instead she applied herself with more fervour to her meal, hoping to finish it before he could drink his tea.

'Have you finished the painting?' he asked pleasantly.

She shook her head. 'Not yet,' she said after she had swallowed.

'I should like to see it again, if you don't mind.'

'There's no point, Mr Marinozzi.'

'Please call me Julio.' His voice dripped seduction. Under the table she felt his hand on her knee. She moved sideways, out of his reach.

'Oh, I couldn't!' she said with exaggerated surprise. 'It is so disrespectful! I mean, you're as old as my father!'

The smile stayed fixed on his face. 'What is age among friends?'

Friends. Oh, God. She put more rice in her mouth. It had lost all its taste and was dry as sand. She'd better stop eating before she choked to death. Her bill was on the table. She took the amount from her shirt pocket, put it on top of the slip of paper and pushed her chair back.

'I have to go now. Good evening, Mr Marinozzi.'

'One moment please, Miss Mitchell.' He reached in his pocket, put some coins on the table and stood up. 'Let me escort you home.'

Linden moaned inwardly. 'It's not necessary. Please finish your tea.' It was useless, of course, Mr Seductiano wasn't interested in tea.

They walked along the busy shopping street towards the wharf, then left. It was obvious he intended to take the short cut along the beach, but she determinedly turned into the village street that led into the general direction of her house. It was a roundabout way, quite a bit longer, but at least there were houses and people.

He put his hand on her shoulder. She stopped, shrugging the hand off.

'Mr Marinozzi, please do not touch me.'

He feigned surprise. 'I was only trying to be friendly. Please do not be offended!'

Without answering she kept on walking, swinging the little plastic carry bag that held the toothpaste. Not much of a weapon. Flat sandals were no good either. Who'd ever thought she might need a can of mace on

Rainbow Island? Or a little panic whistle. Shriek, shriek—help, help.

They came to the last village house. A narrow path led to her and Justin's houses. It was not very long. It was pitch dark. In her haste she stumbled and almost tripped. He took her arm.

'Let me help you.'

She yanked her arm out of his grasp and walked on. Fortunately it wasn't far, but it seemed longer than it ever had. When she reached her house she was breathing hard.

'Good night,' she said in a tone that was barely civil. She started up the stairs.

He followed her up. She opened the door quickly, but she was not fast enough. He was inside, before she could close the door on him. He closed the door behind him and swiftly moved over to the painting and looked at it.

'Miss Mitchell, I am willing to pay you a generous price for your painting.'

'It's not for sale,' she said coldly. She was still standing near the door, ready to leave.

He was not put off in the least. He came slowly over to her, smiling, his eyes directed on her breast.

'I'll pay you a thousand dollars.'

He wasn't lying at least. Generous it was.

'I told you, it's not for sale.' She opened the door. 'Please go, Mr Marinozzi.'

He moved very close to her and put his hand on her hair. She reared back and he smiled.

'I'm not talking about *ringgit*—Malaysian dollars,' he said carefully. 'I mean American dollars.'

She stood very still. One thousand US dollars. It was way out of line. Despite the tropical heat, she was suddenly cold with anger. She glared at him.

'Mr Marinozzi, my painting is not for sale,' she said icily. 'And neither am I.' She took a deep breath. 'And I want you out of my house this very minute, or I'll scream the place down. Out! Now!' She stepped back far enough to give herself a chance to put her threat into action if he made one move in the wrong direction.

He did not. He stood in the open doorway, and gave her an evil look. 'Don't excite yourself, Miss Mitchell. I'm going. But I'll be back.' He turned and went down the stairs into the night.

She slammed the door shut, then locked it and leaned against it, shaking. She closed her eyes. The bastard, she thought furiously. That miserable slithery bastard!

She heard footsteps coming up the stairs. Pounding on the door. Her heart beat in her throat.

'Linden? It's me, Justin. Open the door.'

She felt faint with relief, turned the key and let him in. His hands were in the back pockets of his shorts, his eyebrows drawn together in a frown.

'What was going on here? I heard you slam the door and when I looked out I saw Marinozzi walk away.'

'Sit down.' She lowered herself in a chair and took a deep breath. 'He still wants to buy my painting. He offered me one thousand dollars for it. Not *ringgit*, mind you. US dollars.'

For a moment he said nothing, digesting this in silence. 'I see,' he said then. 'And what did you say to that very generous offer?'

'What do you *think* I said? I told him my painting is not for sale, and neither am I.'

'And then?'

'I told him to get out. He did. However, he promised he'd be back.'

Justin nodded thoughtfully, then pushed himself to his feet. 'I think I'd better take care of our friend before he changes his tactics. Make sure you lock up tight.'

'I don't think he'll try rape,' she said lightly. 'Or he would have tried it earlier.'

'We don't know that, do we?' He wasn't laughing.

'What are you going to do?'

'Make sure he leaves at first light tomorrow morning.' He strode out the door and jumped down the stairs taking three steps at a time. At the bottom he stopped and looked up. 'I'll pick you up at nine in the morning, all right?'

'I'll be ready.'

He disappeared in the direction of the little house Marinozzi had rented. She wondered what Justin would say to the man, how he could make him leave. There was always brute force, of course, but she couldn't quite picture Marinozzi in a fight. He was so out of shape he'd be down and out in a matter of moments. Not that I'd mind that, she thought nastily.

It was only minutes later when Justin came outside again. He strode down the path to his own house, went up the stairs and into the front door.

In the morning they left at nine, walked to the wharf and climbed into Justin's motor boat. Soon they were out on the water.

'Did Marinozzi leave this morning?' she asked.

'Yes. I saw to it personally.'

'He didn't give you any problem?'

'None in the least.'

'I wonder why.'

He shrugged. 'The man is a coward.'

'What did you say?'

He grinned. 'I told him if he valued his looks he'd better get out of my way.'

She couldn't help laughing. 'You'd think anything would be an improvement.' She grimaced. 'That sounded pretty spiteful, didn't it? Well, charity in the face of rottenness has never been my strong point. I guess at heart I'm not really a nice person.'

He nodded. 'Malicious, unforgiving.'

'Hey! You didn't have to agree with me!'

He laughed and she barely controlled the urge to

stick out her tongue at him. She leaned back on her arms, lifted her face in the wind and closed her eyes, 'This feels heavenly. Nothing better than clean sea air.'

But she'd said the same about the air in rural Pennsylvania in spring, when everything was crisp and green and the crops were sprouting and the wind was fresh and clean. Or the air in the mountains—fragrant with the smell of pines.

Sadness swept over her. So many memories were all tied up with Waite. Would she ever be able to think even simple thoughts without feeling this pain?

She opened her eyes and Justin was looking at her and there was no doubt what was in his eyes. She looked away, feeling her heart contract. *I don't want a lover*, she wanted to say. *I need a friend. Please, be my friend*. But it wasn't something you just said out loud. And it probably wasn't possible at all. Many did not believe there could be true friendship between a man and a woman that excluded sex. Maybe it was true. Maybe it was always there in the background, that primitive instinct, drawing them together.

And how easy it would be with Justin. She started at the shape of Penang coming closer and closer.

She felt a hand on her knee and looked up. He withdrew his hand.

'What were you thinking about?'

She hesitated. 'Do you believe non-sexual friendship between men and women is possible?'

'There are many kinds of friendship.'

'I mean a real, close friendship.'

He shook his head slowly. 'No. Not for me, at any rate.' He paused. 'Were you thinking about us in particular, by any chance?'

'Yes.'

He shook his head in disbelief. 'Linden, we hardly have a non-sexual relationship. The fact that we haven't acted on it doesn't make it any less so.'

She didn't answer. Spray splashed over the side of the boat and wet her face. She wiped it off. It was true of course. The feelings were there between them, undeniable. It was only a matter of time. Or a matter of avoiding it by leaving.

They said nothing more until they reached Telok Bahang's fishing pier. Justin jumped out and tied the boat up to one of the bamboo poles. The boat wobbled precariously as Linden stepped on to the side, and Justin held out his hand. She reached for it. She made an unlucky jump and nearly lost her balance, but with an almighty yank Justin practically dragged her on to the pier. She fell against him, laughing, and he steadied her with both arms around her.

'You practically dislocated my arm!' she said accusingly, looking up into his laughing face.

'I know how to fix that.'

'I'm not surprised.'

He was still holding her against him, showing no signs of releasing her.

'I'm steady now,' she announced.

'I'm not finished with you yet.' And with that he kissed her full on the mouth, an outrageously passionate kiss that rendered her weak and motionless. He withdrew without letting her go and held her gaze.

'And that is to warn you not to have any more silly ideas about what kind of relationship we have.' He let go of her then, picked up her suitcase and his own faded dufflebag, suddenly all business again. Her legs no longer steady, she walked behind him along the narrow plank pier to the beach.

'Wait for me here,' he said. 'I have to find out where I should leave the boat. I may be taking up someone else's place down there.'

Ten minutes later, the boat in a different spot, they walked to the road. A *teksi* was waiting, the driver leaning against the door, smoking a cigarette.

'Where did *he* come from?'

'I made arrangements with the hotel to have a taxi waiting for us here. We'll drop off our stuff, have a cup of coffee and go straight into George Town.'

It was strange to be in such luxurious surroundings after more than two months in a simple fishing village. Soft carpeting everywhere. Deep, upholstered chairs. The coolness of air conditioning.

They had adjoining rooms with a two-sided connecting door, which was locked. Standard rooms, nicely appointed, but similar to rooms in a hundred other modern hotels. Stepping into the room there was a bathroom on one side of a narrow passage and a wardrobe on the other. Then a bedroom with a big double bed, two easy chairs and a coffee table, a desk, a chest of drawers, a television set and a small refrigerator. There was soft blue carpeting, heavy curtains to block out the early morning light, plenty of lamps, and an air conditioning going full speed, making the place feel like Minnesota in the dead of winter.

'What do you think?' Justin was standing behind her and she turned around, rubbing her arms.

'Positively luxurious after my humble abode on Pelangi. It's lacking one thing though.'

He raised his eyebrows, 'Oh?'

'A fireplace. I'm freezing.'

He grinned and looked around for the thermostat. 'It's on its coldest setting. 'I'll turn it up.'

'Thanks.'

The coffee shop was partially outside, surrounded by blooming plants and trees, and had a postcard-picture view of the beach and ocean. The small tables were covered with cloths and had a small vase of flowers in the middle. There was a cart with pastries—black forest gateau, rum cake, cheese cake and more. They succumbed to the temptation.

'You know what I'd like for lunch?' she asked, swallowing her last bite of chocolate cake and cream.

'How can you think of lunch with your stomach full of cake?'

'Easy. I'd like a cheeseburger. A big one with lots of cheese and tomatoes and onions and pickles and a double serving of french fries.' She feigned an expression of heavenly delight and sighed longingly.

Justin rolled his eyes. 'You've got to be kidding. Junk food! In a place where they have the best food in the world!' He looked quite outraged and she laughed.

'Listen, I'm only a honky from Pennsylvania. After two months of Oriental cuisine, delicious as it may be, I want a hamburger and french fries.'

He sighed in resignation. 'I imagine McDonald's has found it's way to Georgetown. And if by some miracle it hasn't, the big hotel coffee shops no doubt will have burgers for unimaginative foreigners.'

She gave him a saintly smile. 'I won't take offence.'

'Good. There's cream on your nose.' He leaned over and ran his finger over her nose before she'd taken her napkin off her lap. He licked his finger. 'Mmm . . . tastes like you.'

'You're crazy.'

He nodded. 'I am—about you.'

'You're trying to make me feel bad.'

'I'm not. You don't understand. I'd like to make you feel *good*.' There was humour in his voice, but his eyes were serious.

'Have you been drinking?'

'Yes. Coffee. Come on, drink up and let's go.'

In the back of a taxi he put his arm around her shoulder and pulled her closer. She tried to move away.

'Stop it, Justin, please.'

'What am I going to do about you, Linden?' he whispered. 'I've tried to be the gentleman, but it's not easy, you know. I haven't touched a woman in . . .'

'Spare me! I don't want to hear the details of your love life!'

'What love life?'

She sighed in exasperation. 'It's not my fault you're such a failure in that department. I thought western men liked oriental girls. Why haven't you married one by now? They make wonderful wives. Beautiful, sweet, willing, obedient to your every command.' She spoke in a low voice, not wanting the driver to overhear their conversation.

He nodded. 'It's what's called *boring*. Besides, they giggle too much.'

'Well, you banished yourself to this island. Don't punish *me* for it. Now take your arm away!'

'Relax,' he whispered in her ear. 'What can possibly happen in the back of a taxi?'

'Use your imagination!' she hissed, and he broke away, laughing.

CHAPTER SIX

I haven't been happy like this for ages. It was a conscious thought that came to her as they were walking along a narrow, busy street in George Town eating roasted Chinese chestnuts. They'd bought them from a roadside cart, a whole half-kilo of them in a cone-shaped bag fashioned from a Chinese newspaper.

It felt so good to be happy, to feel this light-hearted joy in being here in this exotic town of dazzling lights and spicy fragrances—to be here with a man who made her laugh.

He kept touching her—holding her hand, putting an arm around her shoulder, wiping hair away from her face. His eyes kept coming back to her, laughing into hers, telling her what his mouth didn't say. And she couldn't help but smile back, relishing his touch.

They'd had their hamburgers for lunch; Justin eating not only one, but two.

'Aren't you ashamed of yourself?' she'd asked. 'Eating hamburgers with all this great food available?'

He looked innocent. 'Why should I?'

'*Hamburgers,* in Asia?'

'What's wrong with hamburgers? Good honest American food for good honest American citizens.'

'So why did you give me a bad time about wanting a hamburger?'

'I did? Why would I do that?' He took another bite which prevented him from saying anything more for the next few minutes, his eyes laughing into hers.

'You're impossible,' she said feebly.

All afternoon they'd explored the town, on foot and in a *trishaw*, telling each other what they remembered of the colourful history of the town.

They'd gone treasure hunting in the junk shops along Rope Walk and found each other Christmas presents—buying them secretly. Among the assorted junk were knick-knacks of all sorts—wood and brass and bone, carved or painted. Old saris and sarongs, chipped Chinese bowls and dishes and spoons, cracked lacquer boxes. In a box full of dusty odds and ends she'd found a small Indian elephant carved of yellowed ivory. It was dusty and dirty, but whole. The carving was delicate and intricate and she could clean it with a toothbrush. She could use the one she had and buy a new one at the hotel drugstore.

She wondered what it was he had bought for her. It seemed heavy. It was roundish, wrapped in newspaper and he carried it in a plastic bag.

'Where shall we have dinner?' he asked. 'What would you like to eat?'

She considered for a moment. 'Something hot and spicy. How about an Indian curry?'

'*Nasi Kandar?* I know just the right place.' He laughed and squeezed her hand. 'I was worried you'd want a hotdog.'

It was late when they came back to the hotel, but the lobby bar was still full of people dressed in their finest, drinking exotic drinks and listening to a three-man band singing Christmas songs.

'How about a drink?' Justin asked. 'Or are you too tired?'

'Me? Tired on Christmas Eve? Never. Just let me shower and change. I'll see you in the lobby bar in twenty minutes. Is that too long?'

'I've never heard of a woman who can shower and change in twenty minutes, but I'll be there.'

She couldn't let him get away with that. In her room she stripped at top speed, turned the shower on hot and soaped herself as fast as she could. Too bad she couldn't stay under longer. A real shower! What luxury. Well, no matter. She could stand under it for the rest of the night after she came back.

From her bag she fished out one of her two good dresses—a sleeveless silk thing that was eight years old, but still looked as nice as the day she'd bought it in Hong Kong for a pittance. It was a beautiful blue-green and had a simple design that didn't age. It hardly wrinkled and was the perfect dress to take along travelling. She slipped it on quickly, put on high heeled sandals and brushed out her hair.

Earrings, where were her earrings? She found them, put them on, and dabbed on some perfume. She examined her face in the mirror, applied eyeshadow, mascara and lipstick in record time and was out the door waiting for the lift with three minutes to spare.

The band was taking a break and there was no music when she arrived in the lobby bar. She searched for Justin in the crowd, hearing around her voices speaking in many languages—French and German and Swedish, or maybe Danish, she couldn't tell the difference. Europeans on the vacation of a lifetime—a trip to the Far East. A group of young Japanese couples, the women quite fashionable, sat around talking and laughing.

She saw Justin at last and began to weave her way among the low tables and chairs, avoiding the tray-carrying cocktail waitresses in their long halter-neck dresses.

He stared at her when he noticed her, as if he wasn't sure what he was seeing. She sat down next to him on the low couch and gave him her most charming smile.

'Linden, you look beautiful,' he said in a low voice.

'Thank you,' she said, humour in her voice. 'Isn't it amazing what a scrap of silk and high heels will do for a girl?'

'Mmm. You keep surprising me.'

'And I even made it in twenty minutes.'

'You certainly did. Miracles never cease.'

He looked good himself. He'd showered and changed as well, wearing light pants and a long, dark shirt with a Mao collar.

'I like your shirt,' she said. 'Very exotic.' *I like your eyes and your nose and your hair,* she wanted to say. *I like those brown hands of yours. I want to touch you. I want to play with your fingers. I want to kiss you.*

'Isn't it?'

'Very.' *What are we talking about?* she wondered, staring at his mouth. There was a moment's silence, then their eyes met and her heart began to double its speed. 'An interesting place this,' she commented casually, staring up at the gargantuan chandelier hanging from the ceiling. 'I'm glad we're not sitting underneath that thing. You never know, it might come down.'

A card listing some of the drinks available stood on the table and Linden picked it up and examined it. 'Listen to those names,' she said. 'Kontiki Sunrise, Desert Dream, Moody Dawn, Penang Fizz, Day Dreamer.'

'Very romantic. Take your pick and we'll order it.'

'What are you having?'

'Scotch.'

'Why so unimaginative? Try one of these.'

'They're much too sweet.'

'All right. Well, I'll try a Day Dreamer. It's rum, Kahlua and orange juice. Sounds good to me.'

The band came back shortly after that, a trio made up of one Malay, one Chinese and one Indian member. It seemed an odd group to be singing *Jingle Bells*, but they did it very well and the guests seemed to love it.

There was a big Christmas tree, all decorated with shiny ornaments and silver tinsel and prettily wrapped packages underneath it, empty boxes probably, but it didn't matter. The place looked nice and the atmosphere was joyous even if it was a public place.

The waitress brought their drinks, kneeling gracefully at the low table to put them down. Linden's drink came complete with a pink orchid and a piece of pineapple, very elegant. It was sweet, but not too strong and she sipped it thirstily as she watched the band and listened to the old familiar songs. It made her feel suddenly homesick, but she pushed the feeling aside.

Justin was playing with her hair, winding it around his finger, smoothing it out again. It felt wonderfully soothing and a wave of fatigue washed over her. She covered up a yawn and he noticed and smiled. 'Tired?'

'Exhausted. And my feet are killing me, I think I have a blister. Do you mind if I go up to bed now?'

'Of course not. It's almost one o'clock.'

'You don't have to go. You can stay.'

'I have nothing against sleep myself.' He paid the bill and took her hand and together they walked to the elevator. He pushed the up button and it came almost instantly.

'That was nice,' she said as the elevator moved upward.

He scrutinized her in the dim light. 'You were looking sad there, for a little while.'

'Not really sad. I feel a little . . . melancholy. I think that's the word.'

The long hallway was deserted and their steps were muted on the carpeting. The doors to their rooms were next to each other and they stopped in front of them. And before she could put the key in the lock, he had taken her in his arms and was kissing her, hard and long, then suddenly withdrew, leaving her breathless.

'Let me have your key.' She gave it to him and he opened her door, then handed it back. 'Would you like me to have a look at your foot?'

She shook her head. 'It's not serious.'

'All right. Good night, Linden.'

'Good night.' She went inside and locked the door. She kicked off her shoes and rubbed her foot. A moment later a knock came on the inside door.

'Linden?'

She went to unlock the door. 'Yes?'

'I forgot to ask you. Do you want breakfast downstairs or up in the room here? We can order now and leave the order form outside the door.' He showed her the form and she looked at it.

'What I'd like is some coffee and croissants in the room and then have a big breakfast downstairs later.'

'Sounds good to me. Then we can exchange our precious presents wrapped in newspaper while we have our coffee. What time?'

'Oh, dear. Right now I feel I could sleep until twelve. I won't though. I wake up at seven no matter what.'

'I'll write down seven-fifteen. How's that?'

'Fine.' It was awkward standing there, with a businesslike conversation covering up all the undercurrents; standing there between two rooms with two large beds while one would have been big enough for both of them. He reached out to her and she did not move away. His face took on a different expression, exposing him, making him vulnerable. Her heart gave a nervous little jerk. She knew what was in his eyes and his thoughts. His hands were on her arms, sliding slowly up to her shoulders, then down around her back. His face came forward. She looked at his mouth coming closer. Everything seemed to move in slow-motion. Then his lips touched hers and her stomach lurched and her blood ran wild. His body was tense with restraint and she felt warm with the knowledge of it, warm too with her own longings rushing through her bloodstream.

It seemed a long time before he withdrew. He looked at her silently and she lowered her gaze, willing her heart to calm down. *No*, she said to herself, *I can't*,

I can't. She took a deep breath and looked into his eyes. 'Good night, Justin,' she said softly.

'Good night, Linden.' He turned abruptly, closing his side of the door. She didn't hear the key turn and she closed her own side, not locking it either.

As she got ready for bed, her eyes caught the little wrapped package on the dresser. She had to clean the elephant yet. She'd forgotten to get another toothbrush. Didn't she have something else she could use? Didn't she have another toothbrush? The one they'd given her on the aeroplane coming over from the States? She rummaged through her cosmetics bag, trying to remember where it would be, and finding it, finally, in a zippered compartment of her travel bag. It was slipped in a see-through plastic sleeve and accompanied by a miniscule tube of toothpaste.

Scrubbing the little elephant with soap and water, she caught her reflection in the mirror above the sink and couldn't suppress a giggle. 'A good thing he can't see me now,' she said out loud to herself, 'naked in front of the sink scrubbing an elephant with a toothbrush.'

Later she lay in bed, looking at the unlocked door, wondering what she would do if he came to her now.

No. Don't think about that.

She closed her eyes and tried to relax. The next thing she knew Justin was sitting on the edge of her bed, calling her name. Her mind fuzzy with sleep, she looked at him, dazed. Light shone through a crack in the curtains. It was morning. She'd been dead asleep all night, never waking once.

'Ah, a sensuous woman,' he whispered, lazy amusement in his eyes. 'Sleeping in the raw.'

The sheet only half-covered her breasts and she yanked it up under her chin. 'You have the rottenest timing! Can't you knock before you come in?'

'I did. You were dead to the world and the coffee is getting cold.'

'You didn't knock hard enough.'

'I didn't want to wake up the entire hotel. There may be a number of people here who wouldn't mind sleeping through the whole of Christmas Day.'

Christmas! She sat up, holding up the sheet with one hand. 'Merry Christmas! Now get out. I'm not decent. Just give me a minute and. . . .'

The rest of her words got smothered by his kiss. The sheet slipped from her hands and her breasts were pressed against his naked chest and she felt the tickle of rough hair. Fire leaped through her and her arms went around him of their own accord and her fingers moved along the strong muscled back.

It was sheer madness. Sheer delicious madness. But he couldn't just come in here and overwhelm her like this. She turned her face.

'Justin,' she whispered breathlessly. 'The coffee is getting cold.'

'To hell with the coffee.'

'Justin, I need my coffee in the morning, or I'm no good!'

It was a very unfortunate choice of words and the breath stuck in her throat when the realisation came. He was laughing against her neck and, suddenly infuriated at her helplessness, she pushed against him. 'Now let me go, Justin!'

'Why are you so uptight?'

'I'm not uptight, I'm mad! You keep walking in on me when I have no clothes on. It's very indiscreet, didn't anybody tell you?'

'I guess not.' He ran the tip of his tongue around her earlobe and she pushed him away.

He drew back. 'What am I going to do with you, Linden?'

'Not a thing!' She drew the sheet back up, and felt an unaccountable wave of sadness wash over her. Tears came to her eyes. 'Oh, get out of here, Justin. Just go!'

He stood up. 'I'll pour you coffee.' With that he strode out of the room.

Linden threw back the sheet, went into the bathroom and splashed cold water on her face. Dressed in her blue caftan, she stood in the doorway a short time later, the elephant wrapped in newspaper in her hand.

'Come in, sit down.' He waved at the chair. The coffee and the croissants were on a tray on the small table. He looked at her, holding her gaze. 'I'm sorry, Linden. I wasn't being fair to you. My baser impulses sometimes get the best of me. I apologise.'

'Never mind,' she said tolerantly, 'it's the animal in you, I quite understand.' She stood in front of him, holding the package in her hand. 'Merry Christmas.' She handed him the package and he took it from her. She sat down again and drank the coffee which was still hot.

He took the paper off and stood the elephant on the palm of his hand, looking with obvious pleasure at the intricately carved piece of ivory. 'It's beautiful,' he said, running his finger over the delicate trunk and tusks. 'An Indian antique, no doubt. Thank you. Now, for you.'

The package was next to his chair and he handed it over. 'And Merry Christmas to you, too.'

It took only moments to take off the newspaper and then she was looking at a brass incense pot, tarnished bluish green and gold. 'This is great! I'll fill it with sand and stick joss sticks in it and put it on my verandah!' She held it away from her a little and examined it. 'I suppose I should polish it. The ones in the temple always are polished, but the colours of the tarnish are beautiful, have you seen? Purple and green and gold and blue. . . .'

'I noticed. Don't polish it if you don't want to.'

'I'll think about it.' She smiled at him, happy with the unusual present. 'Thank you very much, Justin.'

It was a beautiful day. They swam in the swimming pool and later in the ocean. They lay on the beach and played cards and read a book and talked. They sat by the pool in the shade of a large tree, a sea almond, and drank fresh orange juice and one too many Penang Fizzes. They played in the ocean like children and she laughed more than she normally did and she liked the feel of his hands on her body.

Christmas dinner was everything she had hoped for. There were orchids on the table and silver shone on the red table cloths. Beautiful music sounded in the background. The atmosphere was right, the food delicious and Justin was amusing and happy and lighthearted.

She'd spent time and effort on her appearance and she'd seen the admiration in his eyes when he'd come into her room to get her for dinner. She wore the second of her two silk dresses, a simple thing of shimmering white and cream that could go many places and was easy to pack.

She looked at him across the table, realising how well she was getting to know him, how familiar his face was to her and she remembered that first time she had seen him, so long ago, and how infatuated she had been.

He reached out across the table and took her hand.

'Do you remember that Christmas dinner we had on Pelangi?' he asked, as if he sensed her thoughts had gone back to that time. 'The time when my father and I stayed with your family?'

'How could I forget? It was a disaster. The chicken was inedible. The wine was bad.'

He laughed. 'It was the nicest Christmas I'd had in years.'

'It *was* nice, wasn't it? I remember how much we laughed.'

They were smiling at each other, memories in their

eyes, and then the waiter was there filling up their
wine glasses and Justin let go of her hand.

After dinner they sat in the lobby bar for a while,
listening to more Christmas music, sipping Irish
coffee and watching the other guests.

'How about a walk on the beach?' he asked.

She nodded in answer and they rose and walked out
into the night. There were lights in the hotel garden
and they walked past the empty pool over the grass
and on to the sand. There were no other people. The
sky was cloudless and full of stars and a big fat moon,
almost round. It was something out of dream—this
island with its palms and *prahus*, beaches and mosques
and temples and pagodas. How romantic it was here in
the quiet night on the beach with the ocean calmly
washing ashore with soft splashing sounds. Here she
was in a luxurious hotel with the romantic name *Rasa
Sayang*.

Rasa Sayang—the Malay phrase for *Feelings of Love*.

Hand in hand they walked along the water's edge,
not speaking much, just enjoying the peace and
solitude of the quiet night.

They returned to the hotel some time later, and
coming into the foyer bar with its music and light and
laughter was like entering a different world.

'Another drink?' he asked.

She shook her head. 'It's late. Let's just go up.'

They stopped in front of her door and for a long
moment he looked at her silently, then drew her into
his arms and kissed her.

'Linden,' he whispered against her mouth. 'Those
beds in there are awfully big.'

She swallowed. 'I like big beds. I can sprawl all
across them.'

'Come on.' He took her hand and unlocked his door,
drawing her inside.

'Justin, I'm not going to sleep with you.' The words
came out with difficulty.

He switched on the lights. 'Who's talking about sleeping? Those beds are made for watching television while you consume the contents of the refrigerator. Let's see.' He opened the door to the small fridge. 'Red wine, white wine, gin, vodka, scotch. Which one?'

'Red wine,' she heard herself say. I must be out of my mind, she thought. Then she shrugged mentally, kicked off her shoes and sat down on the edge of the bed.

'And what else?' he asked. 'We have smoked almonds, chocolate candy bars, plastic cheese and crackers.'

'Smoked almonds.'

'I like a girl who knows her mind. Catch.' He threw the little bag at her and it fell in her lap.

'Great throw.'

'Bad catch.' He poured the wine in a wine glass, also provided. 'Why don't you see what's on TV?'

She turned the dials. An angry Chinese man with lots of make-up, a long braid and theatrical robes was yelling at some unfortunate inferior. 'A Kung Fu movie in Chinese with dubbing in Malay.'

'Forget it. What else?'

She punched in the next button. 'A weeping woman in a sari—Indian.' She pushed the next channel. Christmas music wafted into the room. 'Bingo! Donny and Marie Osmond.'

He groaned. 'I can't believe it.' He sat down next to her on the end of the bed and handed her the glass of wine.

A commercial break interrupted the show. An English ad for Kentucky Fried Chicken in Kuala Lumpur. A Malay ad for Colgate with a beautiful young Malay couple with stars shooting off their sparkling white teeth.

Wearing white sweaters with green Christmas trees on the front, Donny and Marie were skating, or trying to, in a theatrical winter wonderland on stage.

'They probably taped this show in the middle of August when it was ninety-five degrees,' she said.

'What is this world coming to,' he said in a cracked grandpa voice.

'Would you rather watch Kung Fu?'

'There's a programme guide here somewhere. Let's see what else there is.' The guide had fallen on the floor and he picked it up. 'What day is it today? Oh, here. Well, look at this! Aren't we lucky! This will be over in fifteen minutes and then . . .'

'Dallas,' she guessed.

He shook his head. 'That's tomorrow. Today we have James Bond. *You Only Live Twice*. Have you seen it?'

'No.'

'Good. Neither have I. What kind of movies do you see at home? Horror? Science Fiction? Mystery? Porn?' He sat down again next to her and looked at her with interest as if he were expecting her to spill the contents of her soul.

'I don't. I hardly ever go to the movies. I don't know why. When I do I usually enjoy it.'

Marie was wearing a long white gown and glittering ice crystals in her hair. There was a sleigh with bells and the brightly lit windows of a cottage on a hill.

'Have you been homesick today?' he asked.

'Only a little.'

He put his arm around her shoulder and played with her hair. He liked playing with her hair. Then he leaned a little closer and gently touched her lips and she did not move away.

She should, she knew. Staying here with him was asking for trouble. She should go back to her room and go to sleep. But somehow she wasn't tired. And the prospect of that big empty bed was not inviting.

So stay with him, she told herself.

I can't, she thought, I can't.

The wine glass was still in her hand. In a minute she'd spill it on herself or the bedspread. She drew away. 'My wine,' she whispered.

He took it from her and put it on the desk. He turned back to her and his expression was dark and intense and the laughter had gone. She felt her heart beat frantically in her chest.

'Justin, I had a wonderful day, but I really have to go now.' Her voice sounded strange and it took all her strength not to look away.

'What are you afraid of, Linden?'

She shook her head. 'I'm not sure. I'm just not ready yet. I'm sorry, really I am.' She bit her lip hard, then looked at him again. 'It's not that I don't want to make love, Justin. I do want to. But . . . but I need to know that I'm not doing it because I'm lonely and alone.'

He looked at her for a long silent moment. 'I can't answer that for you.'

'I know.'

'But we are here, you and I, together. Does it matter so very much?'

She nodded. 'Yes.' She looked down on the floor, searching for her shoes. She slipped them on and stood up. He stood up too, standing in front of her, arms folded across his chest, eyes hard. She knew he was angry.

'Linden, when are you going to get over this other man? When are you going to let him stop affecting your life?' His voice was tight and controlled, and suddenly, unreasonably, anger rushed to her head.

'I don't know! Maybe never! And look at yourself! How long has it been since . . . since Kate walked out on you? Years! Did you get over her in two months' time? Well, I'm sorry I ruined your plans for tonight, but . . . but . . .' Her voice shook and she stopped.

He looked at her silently, his face pale. 'It's not just

tonight, Linden. For two months I've seen you almost
every day. We talk. We have coffee or dinner together.
I look at you. I see your face, the way you move, that
gorgeous flaming hair of yours. I listen to you talk and
laugh and every day I'm more in love with you. When
I'm with you I feel . . . different, I feel good, as if life
makes sense again. I want to hold you and kiss you
and make love to you.' He paused, closing his eyes for
a moment. 'And for two months,' he continued slowly,
'I've tried my damnedest to be patient and give you
time. I've tried to understand your feelings, but
now . . .' He shrugged. 'I don't know what I feel
anymore, except that I'm angry and impatient and
frustrated and I don't know what to do next. I kept
hoping you'd forget that other man . . .'

On TV Marie sang sweetly of snow and sleighbells
and he turned and viciously stabbed the button.
Silence fell over the room. She stood near the
connecting door, still and silent, feeling as if
something terrible was happening and she was
powerless to do anything about it.

Justin rubbed his chin, a tired gesture. 'I think
you'd better go now,' he said.

She left without a word, and some time later she lay
in bed, sick with regret and too tense to sleep. From
the next room came the muffled sounds of the
television. He'd turned it on again and was watching
the James Bond movie.

You Only Live Twice. Lucky James Bond. He could
screw up one life and try again. All she had was one
life and she had to live it the right way from the
beginning.

Well, it didn't look like she was doing too well. Had
she made the wrong choices? Should she have stayed
with Waite and help him sort out his life? *Stand by
your man*, was the old adage. At what price? When was
the price too high?

He had hit her in the face. He had belittled her and

disrespected her. Clearly for her the price was too high. Yet it was not easy to let go, to assign him a place in the past marked 'over'. It was not easy to start a new chapter in her life with Justin. Not easy, yet all she had to do was open the door and go in, put her arms around him and tell him she was sorry. He loved her. He wanted her.

But Waite loved her too. She didn't doubt that, not even after what he had done to her. He loved her and he wanted her too. And what was more, he needed her.

I'm not going back to him!

She took a deep breath. 'I'm not going back to him,' she repeated out loud. 'I've done all I can. It's over. Over, over, over.'

She pushed her face in the pillow and moaned.

They left the next morning, after a silent breakfast. A *teksi* took them back to the pier at Telok Bahang. The sea and the sun and the wind in her face were just as they had been two days earlier as they'd boated across to Penang. Now, on the way back, it all seemed different. The world was still the same, but it had lost its charm.

'Thank you for a wonderful time,' she said, after an equally silent walk back to the house from the wharf. 'I'm sorry I made you angry in the end.'

'Let's just forget it. I'm sorry I blew up like that. I should have controlled myself better. Apart from that, I did have a very nice Christmas.' He smiled crookedly and with a wave of his hand strode off down the path to his house, his dufflebag slung over his shoulder.

She walked slowly up the steps and opened the door. The house looked the same. The painting still stood on the easel in the middle of the room. It was good, but she noticed it with a strange sort of detachment. Why am I depressed? she asked herself.

I wish I knew what to do. Maybe I should go home and face up to the world, rather than hide out on this tiny island painting pictures. It's not realistic.

Why not? Justin had been here for three years and seemed to be functioning perfectly well writing his spy novels. So why couldn't she live here and paint?

Because Justin was here writing spy novels.

Oh, damn, she thought, why did he have to fall in love with me? She dumped her bag in the bedroom and sighed. I'm going for a swim, she thought grimly, as if it were some punishment that would exorcise her mind's depressing wanderings.

Walking down the path she heard the faint click-clack of Justin's typewriter floating out of his open window. It hadn't taken him long to get back to work. His desk was in front of the window and if he looked up he'd see her. Not that it mattered. She stubbed her toe on an exposed tree root and cursed under her breath.

There were children on the beach flying hand-made paper kites—brightly coloured birds high in the sky, one orange and blue, the other purple and pink. Lying on her spread-out sarong she squinted up at the sky. The colours were beautiful against the azure of the sky and low at the horizon floated puffy clouds of brilliant white.

There was the familiar feeling of excitement in her stomach as images formed in her mind, the thrill of it spreading through her until she could no longer sit still and her fingers itched for a pencil, a brush, anything. The picture was in her mind, big bright colourful paper birds against the blue and white of sky and clouds. A canvas full of orange and blue and purple and pink. And it wouldn't be gaudy, because she'd make the colours work together.

She jumped up, grabbed her things and ran back to the house. She pulled on a loose shift, found a sketch book and pencils and ran back to the beach. The boys were still there. One of the kites was almost down and she came as close as she could to examine it. The children stared at her. She smiled.

'Your kites are beautiful,' she said in Malay. 'I would like to draw them. Is that all right?'

They nodded wordlessly, then broke out in laughter. They brought the kites down so she could look at them. They were fragile things made of coloured tissue paper glued on to thin bamboo sticks. Practically leaning over her shoulders, the boys watched with fascination as she sketched the shape and contours of the paper birds on to paper.

'Did you make them yourself?' she asked, and they nodded, then began to explain how, giving her details of which she understood little. It didn't matter. She enjoyed listening to their excited voices and their laughter while she sketched, sitting crosslegged on her sarong in the sand. The sun was hot on her head and arms and she knew she should have moved over to the shade of the rain tree. Well, no matter, it was almost done. This was a sketch only.

Back home she realised she had a terrific thirst and her head ached from the heat. Sitting in the hot sun in late morning was a stupid thing to do, but she had her sketch and she couldn't wait to put it on canvas in oils.

Nazirah had made her fish ball soup for lunch, but she could only eat a little, which was a problem because the poor girl imagined Linden didn't like her cooking and she almost burst into tears.

Fortified with two glasses of water and two aspirin, Linden lay down on the bed, the window shutters half closed against the glare of the midday sun.

It was almost three when she woke up. Her headache was gone. She felt great, wonderful. In the kitchen she poured herself a glass of orange juice and drank it. Then she gathered her easel and paints and organised herself in the yard. The light would be good for a couple of hours yet. The temple painting wasn't quite finished yet, but that could wait.

For the next two hours there was nothing but the painting and when finally she went inside, she felt drained, but elated. If only she had better light inside! She could paint the night away.

She lit the kerosene lamp and, frowning, looked around the room. It wasn't really good enough. A pressure lamp would give more light, a lot more light. All right, she'd go out and buy a pressure lamp.

In the fading light she rushed into the village and found what she wanted in one of the shops and brought it home. They were a nuisance, pressure lamps. You poured in kerosene, then pumped them up for several minutes, a boring little job, and then you lit the thing. It gave off a bright white light and an irritating hissing sound.

Well, no matter the sound. There was light now to paint by, even though it was terribly white and glaring. The hours went by unnoticed, until suddenly she realised she was ravenous. It was almost ten o'clock and she hadn't had a thing to eat since lunch. The rest of the fish ball soup was still in the refrigerator and she heated it up and ate it, sitting on her stool, looking at the painting.

She could feel the exhaustion settling on her like a blanket, and she knew there was no way she could paint anymore, no matter how much she wanted to. The hissing of the pressure lamp was getting on her nerves and she turned it off. She cleaned the brushes and went to bed after a hasty shower from the little metal tank. Even the cold water didn't revive her and she fell into an exhausted sleep.

For days she worked on the painting, sometimes for long hours. One afternoon she made the trek to the waterfalls again and swam in the cold stream and sat in the sun. It was good to get away and relax. Her neck and right arm sometimes hurt from working so intensively and the muscles of her back were tight.

It was New Year's Eve and she realised Justin hadn't come to see her since they'd returned from Penang. It seemed strange. She'd seen him go in and out of his house, but that was the extent of it. It was eight o'clock now, and in the dark she quickly went along the path to his house and knocked. The rattling of the typewriter stopped.

'Come in!'

She opened the door and entered, feeling suddenly hesitant. 'Hi,' she said.

He was sitting at his desk, wearing shorts and no shoes. His shirt was unbuttoned and hung loose over his shoulders. It was a hot and muggy night.

'Hi.' He ran his fingers through his hair and leaned back in his chair with a sigh.

'I'm sorry,' she said. 'You're working. I didn't mean to disturb you.'

'It's time to stop. I've been at it all day.' He pushed his chair back and it scraped dully over the wooden floor. He got up and stretched, his long lean body straight and taut. 'Would you like a drink?'

'Please. A gin and tonic.' She looked at his chest covered with dark curly hair.

He went to the kitchen, barefooted, to get the drinks. When he came back a few minutes later he sat down across from her, stretching his legs. She watched him over the rim of her glass, seeing the preoccupied look in his face and the tired lines next to his mouth.

'I haven't seen you for days,' she said.

'I've been working.'

She gathered her courage. 'Are you angry with me? Is something wrong?'

He gave her an irritated glance. 'You know what's wrong. And no, I'm not angry with you. For my sanity's sake it seems best to stay out of your way.' He gulped down his drink and set the glass on the table.

There was a silence. Damn it, she thought, he's not going to make me feel guilty too! She twisted the end of her braid around her finger. He stood up and moved to the window, turning his back to her.

'What have you been doing these last few days?'

'I started another painting.'

'I wondered. I saw the light in your house. You've been putting in long hours.'

'You too, it seems like. How is it going?'

'I'm making good progress.'

'Are you happy with it?'

'I think it's better than the others. What about your painting?'

'Why don't you come and look for yourself?'

'All right. I'll stop by when I get a chance.'

His enthusiasm was touching. Linden stood up, her drink barely touched. 'I'll see you then. Good night, Justin.'

'Good night, Linden.' He didn't try to detain her.

Depressed, she walked home in the warm, starry night. It was New Year's Eve and she was spending it alone in a small fisherman's house on a tiny tropical island in the Indian Ocean.

'Happy New Year,' she said to her reflection in the mirror the next morning. She stared at the bright yellow bikini, feeling anything but bright, anything but happy. Then she grimaced and shrugged, turning away.

Why did she have to wake up so early, this day of all days? Why was she feeling so depressed?

She took a walk along the beach, sat down on a big rock and stared out over the ocean. Nothing but endless miles of water—nothing between here and India. What would it be like to travel by boat and not see land for days and weeks? Such a strange idea. But travelling by boat was a luxury these days, reserved for tourists who wanted fancy cruises with stopovers in exotic places along the way. Not like the old days when colonials would spend weeks on a ship to go from Europe to India or the Far East.

The sea was strangely quiet, almost eerie. As she walked back along the wet sand she noticed how still the water was, like a placid lake with no waves. It floated gently up to the beach, making hardly a sound.

She threw off the sarong and waded into the water. It felt wonderful. The sun was white with heat, no clouds in the sky. For a while she swam, floating on her back now and then, trying to empty her mind of thought. Her stomach growled. She was hungry. Except for a cup of coffee she'd had no breakfast. What time was it? She must have been out for an hour or so. She began to swim back. When the water was waist-high, she began to wade.

Something brushed her leg. A piece of seaweed? She wiped her leg. It was slimy, yuk. She tried to wash it off, rubbing and rubbing it, but it was hard to get rid of it. Out of the water she examined her thigh, but saw nothing, but she could feel a faint, stinging sensation. She shrugged and lay down on her mat to dry off. Soon the stinging became a burning and when she looked again there was a long white streak along her thigh.

The pain was suddenly very bad, a fierce burning as if she'd come into contact with fire, and she jumped up, suddenly alarmed. *What was this? What had touched her in the water?* She began to run, leaving her things behind. She needed something on her leg, something cool and soothing. She clenched her teeth. God, it hurt! Reaching the path, she saw Justin coming down the steps of his house.

'*Justin!*' she called at the top of her voice. He stopped, saw her coming, and waved. She raised her hand. '*Justin!*' She ran, tears of pain blinding her eyes. She stepped on something sharp and it went right into her bare foot. She bit her lip. Damn, oh, damn, she thought.

He was coming towards her fast.

'What's wrong?'

She stopped, breathing fast, and pointed at her thigh. 'I ... don't know.' Her voice squeaked. 'Something in the water ... it hurts, it burns, I can't stand it.'

He took one look and swore under his breath. 'Jelly fish,' he said. 'What the hell were you doing out there in the water?'

The tone of his voice made her forget the pain for a moment. 'What do you mean what was I doing in the water? What do you *think* I was doing? I was *swimming*!'

'Didn't you see?' he said with obvious exasperation. He gestured impatiently at the sea. 'Have a look at the bloody ocean!'

Involuntarily she looked. It was just as she had left it. Smooth and quiet.

'No waves,' Justin continued. 'Don't you know the jelly fish come in close when there are no waves? It throws off their sensory system.'

She turned in anger. 'No, I didn't know that! And stop shouting at me!' She began to walk towards her house, limping on her sore foot, and he took her arm.

'I'll take you to Doctor Chew.'

'What for?'

'It's a big patch. You may need an anti-allergy shot.'

'I'm not allergic to anything and I'm not going to start now!'

'Don't be a damn fool.' He propelled her up the stairs to his house and pushed her down into a chair. 'Sit. I'll get something to put on it for right now.' He produced a tube of cream and gently rubbed it on the patch of white skin. 'It's a tropical anaesthetic. It'll have to do for now.'

'I washed it off as well as I could,' she muttered miserably. 'It wouldn't come off.'

'You ended up rubbing it in more. It's going to be

nasty, I'm afraid. What you really needed was something to deactivate the poison. Bicarbonate of soda or something.'

'Yeah,' she said sarcastically. 'I always carry baking soda, just in case.'

He didn't reply, but straightened and drew her up out of the chair. 'We'll go to your house first so you can put on some clothes. Doctor Chew is close to seventy. I'm not sure his heart is up to seeing you in a bikini.'

'Oh, just shut up, Justin!'

He grinned crookedly. 'And a Happy New Year to you.'

For a moment she stared at him silently. She swallowed. 'Happy New Year.'

Linden got her injection, some cream to put on the affected area, and a warning from the wizened Dr Chew, a minute Chinese with round metal-framed glasses. He was the only doctor on the island and ran his own small, spotless clinic and dispensary, doing everything from delivering babies to emergency appendectomies.

By the end of the afternoon, the white streaky spot on her thigh had turned a pale red. It still hurt considerably, although the cream did give some relief.

Her foot was troubling her too. Something sharp had embedded itself in the sole and she hadn't been able to get it out. She was soaking her foot in hot soapy water when Justin came to the door.

'There's a big jelly fish on the beach,' he announced, then stopped and frowned. 'Why are you sitting with your foot in a bucket of water?'

'It's nothing. Just a little piece of glass or shell, and I can't get it out.'

'You have more trouble than . . .'

'Oh, for heaven's sake, Justin! It's nothing. Don't make a big deal out of it.'

'You're in a fine mood today.'

'And you're not helping. What were you saying about a jelly fish?'

'There's one on the beach, in case you care to have a look at it.'

'On the beach? How did it get there?'

He shrugged. 'Somebody may have dragged him ashore, or maybe it washed up by itself. Now let me have a look at your foot.'

He might as well, she thought. It would save her from contorting herself into more impossible positions. She dried her foot with a towel and deposited it on his knee as he instructed. He picked up the tweezers from the table and took hold of her foot. After the hot water, his hands felt cool.

For not being lovers, she thought out of the blue, he has sure touched and seen a lot of me. Sunbathing in the nude at the waterfalls. In the bathroom after he'd dragged her naked from the mud to his house in the rainstorm. He'd dried and brushed her hair, put cream on her thigh, and was handling her foot right now.

'Ouch!' He was poking around with the tweezers and she gritted her teeth.

'I've got it,' he said, showing her the small piece of shell he'd extracted.

She let out a sigh. 'Thanks. Is it bleeding?'

'Just a little.'

'I'll put a Band Aid on it and then I'll go to the beach to have a look at the monster.'

She'd never seen a jelly fish before, but the size of the thing amazed her. It was a roundish blob of more than a foot in diameter with no discernible head or limbs or tail. It lay in the sand, greyish white, soft and gelatinous, with the sun beating down on it.

'If it belongs in the water, cooking here in the hot sun is a pretty cruel form of torture,' she said.

Justin shrugged. 'I wouldn't worry about it. It's a

pretty low form of life. It has no brain and no nervous system. It feels no pain.'

'It sure knows how to inflict it.'

Justin looked at her thigh. She was wearing shorts to keep it out of contact with cloth. 'It's changed colour,' he observed.

Over the next several days, the spot changed from pale red to pale purple to darker purple. It was ugly and vicious looking and she wondered how long it would take to heal. There was no pain at all anymore, not even when she rubbed across it with her hand. It was numb. Dead. Maybe the poison had killed a whole piece of her thigh. She kept it covered up most of the time and tried not to look at it too much.

Justin had buried himself in his work again. Whenever she passed his house, she could hear the rattle of his typewriter. She seldom saw him, except at a distance. She missed him more than she wanted to admit to herself. So many times she wished she could talk to him, or show him what she had done, or just have a leisurely drink with him. She wanted to know about his new book, but there were no opportunities to ask.

I should go home, she kept thinking. I can't hide forever. I've got to get back and start over. Find a job, face Waite again. Going back to the small town, it was inevitable that she should see him again. She wondered if she could get her old job back. Or maybe she could teach at the high school. Maybe she should move to another town. Philadelphia, or New Orleans, where her sister lived.

But she liked her town, her college, her apartment. She resented the idea of having to give it all up for Waite. But the only other choice was to learn to live with Waite's presence.

As it turned out, the confrontation came sooner than expected. Early one evening she came back from the village and found Waite standing in front of her easel, examining her painting of the kite birds.

CHAPTER SEVEN

TIME froze. Immobilised she stood in the door, clutching the shopping basket, unable to utter a sound. He looked at her silently, standing in the middle of the small room, filling it with his presence. He was still the same man—tall and broad shouldered with the deep inky blue eyes and the untidy curly brown hair. But he looked thinner than she remembered and he looked hollow-eyed and hungry. She realised that she had stopped breathing and she took in air with an audible gasp. His eyes widened and he wiped a hand over his forehead.

'Hello Linden.'

Slowly, very, slowly, she lowered the basket to the floor. There was something very unreal about this scene. It was like watching herself and him as the characters in a movie. She was a doll, a puppet. She didn't feel anything. Except the pounding of her heart and the shaking of her legs.

He took a step towards her and she took a step back. She saw him flinch. Her throat was dry.

'How did you find me?' The words squeezed from her throat in a miserable squeak.

'I was lucky.'

'I can't believe Liz gave you my address,' she whispered.

'She didn't. I went to see her. There was a letter from you on the coffee table. I recognised your handwriting. I wrote down the return address.

'I see.' Why wasn't she feeling anything? Anger, happiness, anything . . . She bent to pick up the basket and carried it to the kitchen. She leaned against the counter and closed her eyes.

This is not happening, she said to herself. I'm imagining it. Waite is not in this house, on this island. I'm suffering from delusions. It's the climate. My brain is growing mildew.

She heard footsteps entering the kitchen. When she opened her eyes he was standing next to her. She stared at his shirt—white with a fine green line. He wore lightweight green slacks. No tie, no jacket.

'Linden . . .' There was a tormented tone in his voice and then her face was against the green-lined shirt, his arms around her. 'Oh, God, Linden, I have missed you so.'

He bent his head and searched for her mouth, kissing her with a desperate passion. For a fraction of a moment she stood motionless, then her senses reeled and emotion washed over her in a wave of memory, filling the frozen void. The feel of him and the smell of him and the familiarity of his body and his touch flooded her awareness. There was nothing but the old sweetness and the loving they had shared and she wanted to hold on to him for ever and ever.

She was crying, tears of some strange emotion rushing down her face and it was all unreal. He kissed her eyes.

'Don't cry,' he said hoarsely, 'please don't cry. I'll make it up to you. I love you, I love you . . .'

But she could not stop crying. The sobbing wracked her body and it frightened even herself. He lifted her in his arms and carried her to the couch, where he put her on his knees and held her to him. She didn't know why she was crying, didn't understand the emotions whirling through her—love and relief and fear and anger in overwhelming strength.

'You hit me!' she sobbed. 'How could you! How could you ever do that to me!' The memory was back, vivid, painful. Again she was lying on the floor, her mouth bruised, her leg hurting, hearing the closing of the door. And suddenly she couldn't stand sitting on his knees any longer. She struggled out of his arms, moved away from him to the other side of the couch and looked at him through tear-blurred eyes. 'How could you?' she whispered.

He shook his head helplessly. 'Linden, I don't know,' he said softly. 'I don't know what happened to me. I've agonised over it, but I don't have an answer. But it won't happen again. I promise. It won't ever happen again.' He reached for her, but she shifted away, shaking her head.

'Don't, Waite. Please don't.'

His hands fell by his side. 'Linden, I want to make things right. I love you. I've gone through hell not knowing where you were, not being able to apologise. I wanted to tell you how much I hated myself for doing what I did. All this time I've thought of nothing else. Please Linden, believe me.' There was so much pain in his voice that she felt her heart contract.

'I believe you.'

Again he wiped his hand over his forehead. 'I know you've put up with a lot from me. I know how difficult it has been for you, and I can't blame you, but please Linden, let's try again. I want to make it up to you. I want to make you happy again.'

For three months he had searched for her, had travelled half around the world to find her, while at home he could have had any number of willing, adoring females. The college was full of them, pretty young girls idolising him. But he didn't want them. He wanted her. He loved her.

She stared at her hands, not knowing what to answer. There was blue paint under her finger nails. On the back of her hand there were pale freckles.

'Say something, Linden.'

She didn't look at him. 'It won't work.'

'We don't know that. We've got to try!'

She shook her head. 'I can't go through it all again.' She stood up, too restless to sit there next to him. It all came back to her, the other side of their relationship. His moods, his depressions, his violent tempers. 'I just can't.' She felt the constriction in her throat. 'I went away as far as I could, because if I didn't, I knew I'd go back to you. And . . . and I just couldn't take any more. You hurt me too badly.'

'I love you, Linden.' He lowered his face in his hands. 'I love you.'

'I know. I don't doubt it, Waite. But it's over now.' She looked away. Darkness was creeping into the room. 'It's better if you go now. You'd better go back to Penang.'

'I'm not giving up that easily, Linden. I can't just go back. I'm going to stay for a while.'

'You can't stay here.' She clasped and unclasped her hands, trying to keep calm.

He stood up, tall and big and overpowering, but the sadness was still in his blue eyes and she felt a rush of despair. His arms came up, then dropped back as if he changed his mind.

'I know,' he said softly. 'I've already made arrangements to stay in one of the houses over there.' He made a vague gesture towards Justin's houses.

She wasn't sure what she felt. Surprise about Waite's uncharacteristic humility. Obviously he had not assumed he could stay with her, taken for granted that she would take him back. But she felt a flash of anger at Justin. Why had he done that? Given Waite a place to stay? How long would Waite stay on now? She didn't want him here. It was difficult to contain her anger and she turned away.

'Please go now, Waite.'

When she looked back he was gone and she heard his steps as he went down the stairs and then she was alone.

She sat down in a chair, feeling numb. Darkness gathered around her, but she did not get up to light the lamps.

Waite was back in her life. And suddenly the numbness was gone and she felt a rising panic.

It seemed a long time later when someone called her name. Her head was resting on her drawn-up knees and it was an effort to raise it. She stared at the shape standing in the open door. It was Justin.

'What are you doing, sitting here in the dark?'

She looked at him, dazed, not answering.

He strode into the room, lit one of the lamps and came towards her. 'Are you all right?'

She nodded. 'Yes.' Her voice sounded strangely husky and she cleared her throat.

He surveyed her, frowning. 'You don't look all right to me.'

'Why did you let Waite stay in one of your houses?'

'I didn't know he was Waite until after the arrangements were made. And even if I had known, I don't believe it is my business to decide whether he is or is not staying on Pelangi.' He turned away and examined the painting of the kite birds.

'You're such a cool number,' she said sarcastically.

He ignored that. 'It's very good, I like it,' he said, meaning the painting. 'What did Waite say of it?'

'He didn't say anything. My painting wasn't exactly the topic of conversation.'

He turned to face her. 'No, I expect not.'

His hands were in his pockets and she noticed they were balled into fists. Maybe not such a cool number after all, she thought with a strange mingling of feelings. She wiped her hair out of her face and straightened her back. 'What did you think of him?' she asked.

He stared at her silently for a moment. 'We talked for a while,' he said then. 'I liked him.' It seemed the admission was made with difficulty.

'Yes. I thought you would.'

'Linden . . .' He came a little closer, a strange look

on his face. He reached out to her, took her hands and slowly drew her up out of the chair.

They looked at each other without moving, just holding each other's hands, as if frozen into eternity. Through the open windows night sounds drifted in on the warm evening breeze—crickets and lizards and other unknown creatures holding their nightly concert. Beyond that was the roar of the ocean.

A strange mood gripped her. On the fringes of her consciousness she sensed his fear, the unspoken questions in his mind. Anxiety curled in her stomach and she was suddenly aware that she was holding her breath. She let it out slowly, feeling the uneasy rhythm of her heart.

Something changed in Justin's face. A muscle jerked in his cheek. His eyes were an impenetrable grey. He drew her to him, pressing her hard against him, bending her head back and kissing her with desperate desire. Her knees buckled and he lowered her to the couch.

'I love you,' he muttered, his hands touching her face, moving down, stroking her breasts. For a moment she wanted to forget everything. Let him hold her and touch her and make love to her. Forget all the pain and misery of the past and drift away into sweet oblivion. And as his hands and mouth moved urgently over her body, fire raced through her, and then fear and anger and confusion.

'Let me go, Justin, please, *please*!'

He lifted her in his arms, carried her to her bedroom and put her down. He leaned over her, kissing her, his hands tearing at her shirt. She was paralysed with the shock. His hands were on her breasts, softly, not rough at all, and his mouth warm and hungry, sent shivers down her spine.

'I want you,' he whispered in her ear. 'Kiss me, Linden, please kiss me.'

She rolled her head from side to side, tears

gathering in her eyes. 'No, no!' She didn't want to be touched, she didn't want those hands on her—not Justin's, not Waite's, not anyone's hands. She felt violated by their desperate eagerness to hold her and touch her as if she were some ... some thing, some possession they could hold and handle at will. As if it didn't matter what she wanted herself. 'Not tonight, Justin. Please, not tonight.'

She felt him go rigid against her.

'What do you mean?'

'I need to be alone.'

He sat up. 'Is Waite coming here tonight?' His voice held barely contained fury. 'What happened when he came here this afternoon? Do you still want him?'

'Justin, please, don't make it more difficult for me than it is already. I just want to be alone.'

'Is Waite coming here tonight?' he repeated.

'No. Not on my invitation, anyway.'

'And what if he does?'

'Nothing! And it's none of your business!'

He held her gaze for a long time and she did not waver. Then he turned abruptly and strode out of the house without another word.

She went into the bathroom and poured cold water over her wrists. She'd come to Pelangi to be alone. Now there were two men who wanted her, two men who said they loved her. She stared at herself in the mirror and a nervous giggle escaped her. Her hair was a mess, there was no make-up on her face and she wore a faded shirt with a streak of orange paint on it. Oh, God, she thought, I'm a sight. What do they want with me, anyway? She suppressed another hysterical laugh and put cold water on her face. Please, God, she said silently, just let them leave me in peace ...

Next morning she packed her back pack and climbed up to the waterfalls. Here she would be alone. Waite would not know how to find her here and Justin would be working, most likely.

She swam in the cold water, and slept for a while in the shade. It relaxed her a little, but when she tried to read, she was still too preoccupied. A troupe of light brown monkeys chattered noisily in a bush nearby, tearing and eating the bright pink blossoms. The ground below the bush was littered with leaves and bits of bruised pink petals.

Walking back home, she knew she was still nervous. Every inch of her body betrayed her state of mind. Her legs moved with difficulty, her stomach felt heavy inside her, her face was tight and her jaws ached. Waite would still be there. He would come and see her again. What could she tell him? How was she going to convince him she didn't want to try again?

But she did not see him for the rest of that day. Her nerves were taut all afternoon and she was too restless to paint. She kept looking out of the window and jumped every time she thought someone was coming up the steps.

She lay awake for hours rehearsing what to say to Waite. It was a useless activity because it would never happen the way the imaginary conversation went. Lying awake worrying about it was non-constructive and a waste of time, but she had no control over it.

She was on the beach the next morning, lying on a bamboo mat, dozing, when a shadow fell over her.

'Hi.' It was Waite, dripping wet, wearing only swimming trunks and a towel slung over his shoulder.

Her heart gave a sickening thud. Why did he have to look so good? Even now she could find no fault with that big, masculine body. She wished he was bow-legged or hunchbacked or chicken-breasted. She wished he had a pot belly or a bald spot or a big nose. But no, he was perfect, this man she'd once loved so much, and his marvellous physique still held its appeal.

'Hi.' She closed her eyes, blocking him out. From the movements and the sounds of shifting sand she knew he was settling himself next to her. She rolled over on her stomach and peered through her lashes. He was sitting with his arms leaning on his drawn-up knees, gazing at her thigh.

'My God, what happened to your leg?'

The day she'd arrived on the island Justin had asked her the same question. The answer then had been different.

'The tender touch of a jelly fish.'

'How did it happen?'

She told him in a few short sentences. She wished he'd go away. Her awareness of his stark male appeal made her uncomfortable. It frightened her to realise how much she still felt for him. But if she got up and went for a dip in the ocean, he'd only follow her. She stayed where she was.

'Did you go swimming?' she asked. Why was she asking the obvious?

'Yes.' He squinted up at the sky. 'This is a beautiful island.'

'Yes.'

'I had a long walk around the island yesterday. I found the Chinese temple on the other side of the village. I'd never seen a place like that. It was fascinating.'

It was an effort not to tell him she'd painted the temple, as she would have some months ago, to talk to him about it and tell him of the difficulties, the technicalities. Now she did not want to speak to him about it. No more closeness or intimacies. It was the only way. No sentimentalities.

'You're going to burn,' she said after a pause. 'You haven't been out in the sun for a long time, you'd better watch out.' His skin was naturally brown, but even he would burn after not having been exposed for months. It was January, and at home the temperatures would probably be below freezing.

'You're right. I didn't think about it.'

'I have some lotion, if you want some.'

'Please.'

She tossed him the bottle and he rubbed his arms and chest with the sun tan lotion. She closed her eyes. She didn't want to look at him.

'Linden? Would you mind doing my back?'

Yes, she answer silently, *I would mind. I would mind very much.* But it was a simple, logical request and she couldn't refuse. She sat up and took the bottle from him. Her hands were unsteady as she squirted some lotion on his back. *It's just a back*, she told herself as she began to smooth it over his shoulders and down his back. *Nothing special, just an ordinary back.* There was a small birthmark under the left shoulder blade, insignificant but familiar, and she tried not to notice, working as swiftly and impersonally as she could. But this was no ordinary back. It was Waite's back and she knew every inch of it, would recognise it out of hundreds of other backs—the feel, the shape, the small birthmark. It was all intimately familiar.

She dropped her hands and screwed the cap back on the bottle.

'Thanks.'

'You're welcome.'

'Linden?' There was a plea in his voice. 'Do we have to be so polite?' His eyes were a deep blue and she averted her gaze.

'I'm sorry. But it hasn't been so easy for me these past few months. I hadn't expected to see you here.'

'I had to find you.'

She didn't reply and a silence hung uncomfortably between them.

'I'd better put some cream on your back,' he said at last.

She shook her head. 'No, I don't need it.' She didn't want him to touch her, to feel his hands on her body. The thought terrified her, and it angered her to still have so much fear for what she might feel for him.

'Linden, you're being silly. Come on.' He leaned over to pick up the bottle and she jerked upright.

'I was just going in. I have work to do.'

He dropped the lotion back on the mat. She got up and gathered her things, trying not to see the pain in his face.

'I'd like to see what you've painted here,' he said.

'You wouldn't like it,' she said stonily.

There was a slight pause. 'I'm sorry I was so critical of that painting you sold.'

She straightened her back and looked directly at him. 'It's not criticism I mind, Waite. It's petty jealousy. You meant to hurt me.'

She saw him wince. Clutching the mat and the towel to her, she walked off through the hot sand, her feet burning. How could she ever again freely share the joy of a good painting with him? The satisfaction of a sale? She'd always worry if he were jealous of her. No matter how bad the painting was in his eyes, if he'd loved her enough, he'd have been happy with her for her success.

She wished there were a way to avoid him, but it was impossible. He lived too close and the island was too small. The next morning she went into the village to buy fruit in the *pasar*, and he saw her leave and joined her. They talked politely, making meaningless small talk. Later that afternoon she went for a walk along the beach and he appeared by her side from nowhere.

She began to hide in the house. From her window she could see him take solitary walks, or sit on his verandah, reading.

Once, when she thought he had gone to the village, she escaped from the house and walked along the beach, feeling like a prisoner out for the first time in years. Not until she was close did she see him perched on the big rock, the highest boulder of the rocky outcrop. Arms leaning on his knees, he sat staring out over the ocean. His back was turned to her and he couldn't see her.

He looked lonely and forlorn and her heart ached for him. Her stomach cramped as she turned and walked away from him. It took more effort than she wanted to admit to herself. She rubbed her stomach. Was it nerves? Hunger? Eating seemed impossible these days, and sleeping was difficult at best. Her nerves were getting the best of her. If only he would leave, she thought. *If only he would leave!*

He'd not come to her house for several days, but one evening he appeared at her door while she was trying to finish the kite-bird painting by the light of the hissing pressure lamp.

Her heart began to race nervously and she stared at him without speaking, holding the wet paint brush in the air.

'May I come in?'

She nodded in answer and stepped aside. He walked over to the painting and scrutinised it for a few silent moments. 'It's good,' he said then. 'Excellent composition.'

'Thank you.' His praise meant nothing now. He's only trying to make me happy, she thought bitterly. She put the brush in a jar of turpentine. With him watching she wouldn't be able to make another stroke.

'I didn't mean to interrupt.'

'I've done enough.' She wiped her hands on a rag with turpentine.

'I'd like to talk to you,' he said, turning away from the painting.

She put the rag down and looked at him. She didn't offer him a seat. She didn't want to talk. She wanted him to leave.

'How long are you staying on Pelangi?' he asked.

She shrugged. 'I don't know.'

'Are you planning to go back home in the forseeable future?'

She lit the kerosene lamp and turned the pressure lamp off. The hissing stopped and the room was awkwardly silent.

'Eventually I'll have to. I can't stay here forever.'

'Will you come back to Pennsylvania?'

'I haven't decided. I still have my apartment, but no job.'

'You can have your old job back.'

'I think it would be better if we didn't see each other every day, Waite.'

He raked his hand through his hair. It was longer than she'd ever seen it. She wondered if he'd entrust his hair to one of the local barbers who set up shop on the side of the road every morning. I'm getting nasty, she thought. Why am I doing that?

'I want you to come back, Linden. I only employed a temporary replacement to finish out the fall term. Your job is open. You can start again on the twenty-third.'

She shook her head. 'No, Waite.' She wondered what had happened to this man. She didn't know him like this—quiet and desperate, with his heart in his eyes.

'Linden . . .' He came forward and she backed away, but he kept coming, reaching for her.

'Don't,' she whispered. 'It's no use. Please believe me. I wish you'd leave. It would make things easier for both of us.'

'I can't leave,' he said huskily, taking her hands.

She pulled her hands loose. 'You'll have to! I'm not coming back to you, Waite.'

There was raw pain in his eyes. 'I love you, Linden.'

'It's too late!' Despair rose inside her. 'It's too late! Don't . . . don't you understand?' To her horror her voice shook.

'Don't say that, Linden. Please don't say that. I need you.'

'And what about me? What about *my* needs? I needed support in my work and career! You didn't give it to me! You belittled me! I can't sacrifice my sense of self-worth, my self-respect. Not for you, not for anybody, Waite!' She took a deep breath. 'I like painting. I like what I'm doing. I have no illusions about being extraordinarily talented, but I do need some respect for what I am from the man in my life. You didn't give it to me. You did not respect me. You *used* me!'

He shook his head. 'No, Linden, no. That's not true.' He reached out to her again and she moved away. 'Don't touch me! *Don't touch me!*' Her voice rose in fear. He paid no attention this time and he was too fast for her. She was in his arms, his mouth on hers. She could feel the trembling of his body as he pressed her against him. He kissed her hard and long until finally she wrenched her head sideways, gasping for breath. 'Let go of me,' she whispered fiercely. '*Let go of me!*' Then she heard the steps on the stairs and Justin stood in the door.

'Take your hands off her!' The icy cold fury in his voice startled her. Her knees were shaking. She glanced at Waite. His face looked pale. His arms were still around her and for a moment he stared motionless at Justin. Then slowly he lowered his arms and took a step forward.

She thought her heart would stop. *They'll kill each other* she thought in panic. Oh, God, please don't let them start anything. She could only see Waite's back, but she could imagine what was in his eyes. His arms hung by his sides, the hands clenched into fists. And Justin, his legs slightly apart, his eyes leaping with anger, looked ready for anything. The air shivered with tension and the silence was suffocating.

For endless minutes the two men faced each other,

neither one making a move. Then Waite's shoulders relaxed. He turned slowly and looked at her for a fleeting moment. Then he crossed to the door, past Justin and went down the stairs.

Justin advanced further into the room. 'Are you all right?'

She nodded, swallowing with difficulty.

'Did he hurt you?'

'No.' She wiped the hair out of her face. 'If you don't mind, I'd like to be alone now.'

The watchful brown eyes scrutinised her closely. 'Why don't you come over to my house for a drink?'

She shook her head. 'No, thank you. Not tonight.'

'Tomorrow night?'

'All right, thank you.'

He didn't immediately go, but stood there, regarding her for a long moment. 'If you need me, you can come to me any time, Linden,' he said quietly.

There was a lump in her throat. 'I know. Thank you.' She'd only seen him once since Waite's arrival, as if he'd kept away from her on purpose.

'Lock the damned place up,' he said, then turned away abruptly.

She watched him as he jumped down the stairs and walked back to his own house, his strides long and unhurried. When she glanced at Waite's house, there was no light. Everything was dark. She wondered where he had gone.

The next morning she saw him go to the beach for a swim, but he did not approach her again for the rest of the day.

She should eat, but when dinner time came she had no appetite. Looking around the kitchen dispiritedly, she wondered what to have. There were eggs and fruit and bread and freshly ground peanut butter that Nazirah had bought in the market that morning. Oil was floating on the top and she screwed the lid back on the jar with disgust. She peeled a banana and ate it.

She wished she hadn't promised to have a drink with Justin. She needed a bath and a change of clothes and it seemed too much trouble.

But the cold water refreshed her and she stood in front of the clothes closet wondering what to put on. Local style was good enough, she decided, pulling out a green blouse and a green and white sarong, which she wrapped around her waist. It looked nice, hanging down to her ankles, tight around her hips. She brushed out her hair and pulled it away from her face with the tortoise shell combs. All that was left was to slip into her sandals and she was ready. She went slowly down the path to Justin's house, noticing from the corner of her eye the light on Waite's verandah. He'd be there, reading. He would see her going to Justin's house. There was nothing she could do about it. She didn't mean to hurt him, or make him suspicious. Enough hurting had been done already, but she couldn't help it. Quickly now she rushed up the steps, knocking on the open door before she went in. Dark head bent, Justin was sitting at his desk, reading through his manuscript.

'I'm sorry. Did I come too early?'

'I was just waiting for you.' He put the papers down and pushed himself to his feet. 'Gin and tonic?'

'Please.' He seemed so calm and controlled, moving easily as he made for the kitchen.

'Come with me while I pour it,' he invited.

She followed him. A moderate supply of bottles stood on the corner of the counter. From the refrigerator he took a bottle of tonic and a lime. 'There's a knife in the drawer. Cut off what you like.' He handed her the lime and his hand touched hers. It was deliberate, she knew, and his eyes held hers for a moment. She felt a tingle in her blood and looked away, uncomfortable.

He poured gin into her glass and filled it up with tonic. She found a knife and a cutting board and sliced off a piece of the lime, then squeezed it into her glass. It slipped from her fingers before she was finished and her trembling hand touched the rim of the glass and it fell over on the counter, spilling the drink, but not breaking.

'Oh, damn, I'm such a klutz,' she muttered, picking up the glass and wiping the rest of the drink down the sink. 'I'm sorry. I've got the jitters lately.'

'So it seems.' He took the glass from her fingers and put her face in his hands. 'I don't like what I'm seeing, Linden.'

She stood very still, her eyes on his. Her heart began to hammer and she felt a quickening of her pulses. His thumb caressed the edge of her lower lip, and she twisted her face away.

'Please don't, Justin,' she whispered.

He lowered his face and his lips touched hers very briefly, then he released her.

'I'll pour you another drink.'

She looked at his hand holding the bottle. A strong brown hand with fingers that knew how to touch gently. She wished she wouldn't think these things. She turned abruptly and left the kitchen.

Back in the living room, Justin sat down next to her on the couch.

'I've decided to go back home,' he said. 'I think it's time.'

'Oh! When?'

'As soon as my book is finished. Another month or so. I'll take the manuscript to New York myself. My editor seems to think it's time for me to come out of hiding. My agent is of the same opinion. He's working on a movie deal for my last book and I'll need to be there. They want to do some publicity for this one, and . . .'

'A movie deal?' She practically gaped at him. 'That's fantastic!'

He grinned. 'I was rather bowled over myself.'

'You're going to be famous.'

'Only *if* they make the deal, and only *if* the movie is a success. I'm counting on nothing.'

'Are you going to live in the States for good?'

He shrugged. 'What's for good? I hope to have a long life ahead of me. Very boring to plan it all out ahead of time. I'm sure there will be times that I want to go back to Pelangi for a while. A reprieve, a vacation, whatever. I don't know what's in the future. I don't even *want* to know.'

'Do you ever think about being a reporter again?'

'Not really. It's behind me now. I think I'll leave it to others.'

She drank her gin and tonic, feeling very thirsty. 'What about the houses?'

'I'll sell them. I know some people who are interested.'

'Who? Foreigners?'

'Oh, no. Islanders.'

She sighed with relief. 'I'm glad. You'll keep your own?'

'Yes. I want to be able to come back whenever I feel like it.' He drained his glass. 'How about another drink?'

'Please.'

But the second drink was a mistake. By the time she had finished it she felt awful. A banana was not dinner, and lunch had been negligible. She straightened in her chair, trying to look alert. But Justin was not easily deceived. His observant eyes missed nothing.

'What's the matter?'

She might as well confess. She sighed. 'I don't feel very well. My head is swimming. I shouldn't have had that second drink.'

He frowned. 'Two gin and tonics shouldn't do that.'

'I hardly had anything to eat today.' She stood up. 'I'd better go home.' But her legs felt rubbery underneath her and the room swirled around alarmingly.

'Sit. Don't move.' He pushed her down. 'You need something in your stomach.' He strode out of the room and returned a short while later with a cup of coffee and two slices of toast.

'How do you make toast without electricity?' she asked.

'In a non-stick frying pan on top of the gas ring.'

'I didn't know you could do that. You're so clever.' She examined the toast. 'It does look funny.'

'You can't have everything. It tastes fine. Eat up. I won't have you passing out in my house if I can help it.'

'I've never passed out in my life.'

'I wouldn't want you to start it now.'

She made a face at him and bit into her toast. She felt better after she had eaten and the coffee tasted good. He was watching her as she ate.

'No wonder you have the jitters. You don't eat.'

'I don't seem to have an appetite any more. I don't know why. Maybe I have some tropical amoeba doing unthinkable things to my insides.'

'I doubt it,' he said drily, 'the creature troubling you is six feet tall and speaks English.'

Maybe even two of those, she thought, but didn't say it. She drank the coffee and put the cup on the table. 'Thank you. That was nice.'

'Why is he still here?'

'He's trying to win me back.'

He looked at her intently. 'From what I've seen he hasn't made much progress.'

She stood up. 'He's a persistent man.'

He stood up too. 'Are you scared?'

She swallowed. 'Yes.' She turned and walked to the door. 'I'll go now. Good night, Justin.'

'I'll walk you home.'

'I'll be all right.'

'I'd rather just be there when you go down the stairs and up yours.'

'I'm not drunk, for heaven's sake.'

'I didn't say you were. But you were sure looking green there for a moment.'

She followed him down the stairs. She was still feeling a little giddy, but nothing much to worry about. He waited for her to go into her house, then turned to go back. He hadn't attempted to touch her or kiss her. When she looked out the window she saw Waite still sitting on the verandah.

The next morning she woke to the sound of someone pounding on her bedroom door.

'Who is it? What . . .'

'Justin,' came the short reply. 'Are you decent?'

'What do you want?'

The door opened and his head appeared around the corner. 'I'm cooking you breakfast this morning. You have ten minutes to get yourself to the table.'

She pulled the sheet over her head and groaned. 'I don't want to eat.'

'You'll have to force yourself.'

'I'll get sick.'

'No you won't. Nobody ever got sick on my omelettes.'

'Oh, leave me alone!'

'My mistake has been that I've left you alone too much. Now get out of bed or I'll give you personal assistance.'

'You would too, wouldn't you?'

'Absolutely.'

She gave a martyred sigh and sat up, clutching the sheet to her chest. 'All right, all right. Go do your thing in the kitchen.'

'Your graceful acceptance of my generous offer is most touching.'

'Get lost!' She picked up her pillow with one hand and threw it in his direction. He caught it neatly and

tossed it back at her. His aim was superb. It would
have hit her right in the face had she not grabbed it
with both hands, an automatic gesture that resulted in
the sheet slipping down to her waist. It took a fraction
of a second to realise she was sitting there in all her
bare-breasted glory clutching the pillow in front of her
face. She lowered it, covering her chest, and noticed
Justin's smirk.

'Great catch,' he said, closing the door behind him.

Linden made a face at the closed door and slid her
legs over the edge of the bed.

It was not such a terrible ordeal after all to eat a
decent breakfast. The omelette Justin made was light
and fluffy and delicious, and her stomach did not
object in the least.

'Thank you,' she said when she was finished. 'That
was very good.'

'You're welcome,' he said with an exaggerated bow
of his head. 'And now I've got to get back to my
miserable little manual typewriter. Take one guess as
to what I'm going to buy as soon as I'm back home.'

'An electric one.'

'Wrong. I'm going to get me a word processor. No
more fooling around with primitive typewriters.'

'I'm impressed. Computers intimidate me no end.'

'If you can type, you can use a word processor.'

'Give me a manual brush and a few pots of primitive
paint any time.'

He smiled into her eyes. 'All right, it's a deal.'

And before the meaning of his words sank in, he
had left.

Waite brought her flowers the next day, a huge bunch
of orchids of various kinds—large pink ones and
smaller white ones and sprigs of tiny yellow ones in
clusters. It was a typical Waite gesture—extravagant,
embarrassing.

'Thank you,' she said. 'They're beautiful.' Which

was the truth. Now what was she going to do with them? There wasn't a vase in the house. There were some empty glass jars and a brown-and-yellow can that had contained KLIM milk powder. He watched her as she arranged the flowers in the various containers, then followed her into the living room where she put the orchids on the coffee table and the book shelves.

'Orchids in a jam jar. Good title for a book,' she said. 'Or for a movie.' She was standing with her back turned to him, looking at the flowers on the shelf. The next moment she felt his arms around her, turning her towards him, holding her tightly.

'I can't take any more, Linden,' he said hoarsely. 'I can't stand not touching you. You're beautiful. I love you. I want you.' He began to kiss her feverishly and she wrenched her face away.

'Stop it! Waite, *stop it*!'

'Last night you were at Justin's house for hours. I thought I was going crazy. What is it between him and you?'

She stood rigidly in his arms. 'Let me go, Waite.'

'No. I'm not! Answer me!'

'I don't owe you an answer! I don't owe you anything!'

There was a silence. He was fighting with himself, she could tell. She felt sick.

'Linden,' he said softly, 'please come home with me. We'll start over. We'll get married if you like. Everything will be better, you'll see.' His voice was so persuasive, his eyes so full of promise and love. 'As soon as the weather gets better we'll go camping in the mountains again. We'll go to New York for a long weekend.'

She closed her eyes for a moment. 'Please, don't do this, Waite. I told you, it's over. Please, please just leave me alone.'

His hands were in her hair, winding it around his hands and she was trapped. He pushed her face back and kissed her again, pressing her against him. She tried to keep herself as rigid as possible, not to respond to his kisses. He let her go eventually.

'I thought you loved me,' he said bitterly.

'I did.'

'Can't you forgive me? It happened once. Only once!'

Once is too often! She took a deep breath, relieved to be free of his embrace. 'Maybe in time I can. But I can't forget, Waite. I can't ever forget what you did to me.'

'Give me another chance. I'll do anything. Just one more chance.'

'It wouldn't solve anything, don't you see? Nothing will change. You will still be unhappy about your job, about your students, about your painting. You'll take it out on me again, sooner or later. And I can't take that risk. I have to take care of myself, Waite. I've stuck by you as long as I could, but I can't do it any more. I've asked you to get help and you refused. I'm sorry, but I just can't take any more.'

She wished she could ignore the despair in his eyes, the helpless way he ran his hand over his forehead.

'I'll promise everything will change. I promise.'

She shook her head. 'You've said it before, and it only got worse. You resent it when I sell a painting. You don't like my work and you're always criticising me. I can't live with that. My self-respect and my ego are not up to that kind of treatment. You scare me with your anger and your depressions.'

'It wasn't always like that! We had *good* times! I keep thinking about the good times. I keep thinking about holding you again, loving you . . .'

'Don't, Waite, please don't.' Tears came to her eyes. Why was it so painful to remember? Why was there still this deep aching longing to have back what they once had? How long would it take before she would be free of it all?

'If you loved me . . .'

And suddenly something snapped in her and the words echoed in her mind. *If you loved me . . . if you loved me . . .* Her hands clenched into fists with anger. It rose in her like a hot ball of fire.

'*If* I loved you! Oh, don't give me that, Waite! I did love you! I loved you more than you'll ever know! Why do you think I stuck it out with you for such a long time? Why do you think I didn't walk out on you earlier? Well, I had to save myself, Waite. I was drowning. And when you hit me, something died in me. I've never felt so humiliated and degraded in my life! Nobody hits me, Waite. *Nobody!*'

'I don't think you ever loved me,' he said bitterly.

She went wild with fury. She was trembling on her legs with the force of it. 'How *dare* you say that? After all I went through with you!' A sob broke in her throat. 'Get out! Just *get out!*'

He didn't move. 'Tell me you don't love me anymore.'

In the silence she could hear the beat of her own heart.

'I don't love you any more,' she whispered.

But he didn't leave. Not the next day or the day after that. He did not come to see her anymore, but she knew he was there in the house. He took long walks all over the island. He lay on the beach and acquired a tan. He looked beautiful, except for his face which was old and sad.

She could not stand it any longer. His presence dragged at her spirits. She would watch him from her window and her heart ached.

Justin came to see her every day now, saying little, just looking at the progress of her paintings, and looking at her.

Checking up on me, she thought wryly. Making sure I'm still in one piece.

'What's going on?' he asked one day.

'Nothing.'

'You look like hell. He looks like hell.'

'I'm sorry if it disturbs your sense of aesthetics.'

His eyebrows rose in faint surprise. 'Well, this is another side of you. Lady Sarcastic. Why is he still here?'

'I have no idea.'

He straightened. 'All right, I think it's time somebody took action.' He made for the door.

'What are you going to do?'

'I'm going to get rid of him.'

'I thought you said it wasn't any of your business.'

He turned and looked at her. There was a tense catch at the corners of his mouth. 'I'm making it my business.'

'Why?'

'Do you have to ask?' And with that he leaped down the stairs.

The next morning Waite was gone. It was the second man Justin had sent off the island because of her.

The relief that followed Waite's departure was incredible. She felt free again. Free to go out at any time without fear of running into him. Free to paint again. Suddenly she could eat again. At night she slept soundly and she woke up in the mornings feeling ready for the day.

But Justin had stopped coming to her house again and she saw little of him. At night his light was on until all hours and she knew he was finishing his book.

It was time to go home.

CHAPTER EIGHT

THERE seemed to be no reason to stay any longer. Even on this small island she'd found no peace. She'd go back home and move to another town. Maybe New Orleans, where her sister Stefanie lived. At least now she knew she could not go back to her own apartment, back to the college. She'd have to start over somewhere else.

She'd find another job. Drown herself in work. Start a new life. New friends. No emotional ties.

First she had to finish both the paintings. She still owed one to Justin. It had been days since she'd last spoken to him. He was busy finishing his book, but that wasn't the only reason, she was sure.

He was at his desk when she knocked on the open door.

He looked up from his typewriter. 'Come in.'

'I've decided to leave too,' she declared without preamble.

'Where will you go?'

'I'll stay with my sister and her brood for a while. Her baby is due soon and I imagine she can use some help.'

'You're not going back to Pennsylvania?'

'Only for a couple of days to pack up.'

'I see.' He looked down on the pile of typewritten pages, his thoughts obviously elsewhere. There was a slight pause. 'When will you leave?'

'In a few days. Friday, or Saturday.' She was standing near the door, leaning against the wall. He came to his feet and gestured at a chair.

'Sit down.' He lowered himself in a chair across from her. 'You know, Linden, that I'm not going to let you disappear from my life.'

She swallowed. 'Justin, this is not a good time for me. I need to get myself together . . .'

'I know. I understand.' He paused. 'I have a proposition. Let's meet in New York three months from today.'

She nodded. 'All right.'

'Good.' He leaned back in his chair. 'And now something else. I want to buy one of your paintings.'

'You don't need to. I owe you one. You can have whichever one you like—the Chinese temple or the bird-kites.'

'If you don't mind parting with them, I'd like them both. I'll pay you for one.'

'Why do you want them both?'

'Because I like them. Because I've seen you paint them, because they're yours.'

'You may get yourself some inferior work on your walls.' She couldn't hide the bitterness in her voice and Justin gave her a sharp look.

'I'm not bothered what the so-called experts say, Linden. No one needs to tell me what I like or don't like. I'm quite capable of deciding that for myself. Besides, I'm not exactly the first one to buy your work.'

'No.'

'Waite obviously has problems, and they have nothing to do with you. His opinion is only his opinion and nothing more. It does not change what you really are, what you know yourself to be, unless you let it.'

'I know. But sometimes it's hard not to be affected by someone's opinions.' She attempted a smile. 'I'd like you to have my paintings.'

'Thank you. Are you sure you don't want to keep the temple? You did say it wasn't for sale.'

'It wasn't. It isn't. I'll give it to you in return for Christmas on Penang. A good time like that isn't for sale either.'

There was warmth in his eyes and she looked down on her hands. 'I should have stayed with you that night,' she said softly.

'No,' he said slowly, 'no you shouldn't have.' He stood up and came to her chair, reaching for her. 'Come, let me hold you for a while.'

She stood in his arms, her face against his shoulder.

'No matter how much I've wanted you all this time,' he said quietly, 'I'm glad now that we haven't slept together.'

She raised her face in surprise. 'Why?'

He gave a funny half-smile. 'At least now I know that to you it means more than just a good time.'

She said nothing to that.

'At first I had no patience for your grieving for a man who hit you and treated you badly. But I know now that what you give you do not give easily and it's harder to give up and it hurts more. And whatever you may give me in the future I will value more.'

She didn't know what to reply, but she felt warm with gratitude and wonder, and other feelings yet too delicate to name. He lifted her face and kissed her and she responded without restraint. Then he released her abruptly and turned away.

'I'm sorry,' she said, 'I didn't mean to . . .'

'But you do, you know, every time.' He gave her a rueful little smile. 'That's why I keep away from you.'

'I think I'd better go then.'

'Have some coffee first. That should be safe enough. Just don't kiss me anymore.'

'You started it.'

'I did. I should know better. Come on, help me in the kitchen.'

He put water on the gas ring to boil. 'What are you going to do with your house?'

'Oh, yes, I wanted to talk to you about that. I think I want to sell it.'

'Are you sure?'

'I can't keep it up very well all the way from the States. And I don't know when I'll have the money again to come out here.'

'Would you like me to sell it for you?'

'Would you?'

He smiled. 'I would.'

But it was not so easy to leave after all. It was Thursday evening and everything had been taken care of. She was packed except for the clothes she had on and the ones she'd wear in the morning. The fridge was empty and turned off, the food eaten or given away to Nazirah.

She'd refused Justin's offer of dinner and had eaten in the village one last time—*mee goreng* from Mak Long Teh's cart. Now the only thing left to do was to say goodbye to Justin.

He was waiting with a bottle of wine. The atmosphere was strained and they talked about practicalities while they drank it. Did she have something warm to wear? he asked. Yes, she said, she had a jacket, and besides, her friend Liz would meet her at the airport with her winter coat. Were all her papers in order—tickets, passport . . .

She would stay with Liz while she packed up her apartment and put her belongings in storage for the time being. Then she'd drive to New Orleans.

She was drinking her wine too quickly, aware of his eyes that were looking at her all the time. Her hand trembled. She hated saying goodbye. She dreaded the moment she'd have to get up, say the final words, and leave.

Not wanting to prolong the awkwardness she'd not wanted Justin to take her to Penang in his boat. Instead she'd made arrangements with an old fisherman to ferry her across.

Justin was sitting next to her and touched her hair. It was the first time this evening he had touched her.

'Why are you so nervous?' he asked.

She swung her hair back over her shoulders and attempted a smile. 'I hate saying goodbye. I'm scared. I don't know what I'm doing anymore.' *Maybe I don't really want to leave you.*

But she must, for her own safety.

'You're going to your sister. You're going to relax. Paint. Enjoy New Orleans. And in three months minus four days you'll come to New York.'

He's given her the name and address of his agent, who would know where to contact him.

'Where will you be?'

He shrugged. 'Who knows? In a hotel, an apartment. I don't know. I'll have to see what the housing situation looks like when I get there.'

'Maybe you'll be in California working on the screenplay.'

He laughed. 'I don't believe it will develop that fast, if at all. Anyway, if I'm not in New York, I'll let you know.'

Her throat dry, her knees trembling, she stood up.

'All right, I'll see you then, wherever you may be. I'd better go now. I . . .'

The rest of her words were silenced by his mouth. He kissed her fiercely and she clung to him with a sudden wave of overwhelming emotion. He pulled her shirt loose and slipped his hands under it, spreading them against her bare back.

'Linden,' he whispered, 'let me touch you. I want to see you one more time.' He drew back a little and, looking into her eyes, he slowly unbuttoned the blouse and slipped it off her shoulders.

She stood very still, the blood pounding in her head, feeling the gentle touch of his hands on her breast. His hands moved up, sliding slowly along her neck and jaw to her mouth, tracing a finger along her lower lip. 'You're beautiful,' he said softly. There was love and desire in his eyes, and something else—sadness maybe.

His hands were moving, touching, caressing her everywhere and all the while he kept looking at her and the tension became palpable in the room.

She put her hands on his chest, feeling the fabric of his shirt under her fingers and she began to work the buttons through their holes until she could put her hands on the bare brown skin underneath. Under her fingers she noticed the heavy beating of his heart. They came together again, mouths clinging and he led her to the couch and she lowered herself, closing her eyes. He leaned over her, his mouth on her breast, and her face was in his hair and she smelled the clean warm scent of it.

Three months she'd been on Pelangi—three months of hearing his voice, seeing him smile and, seeing the muscled beauty of his brown body. But she had not consciously wanted to see him because her mind had been too full of another man, too full of pain. Now she was in his arms, touching and kissing, knowing he wanted her, knowing she wanted him too. And suddenly there was the terrible fear of loss, and a need, a longing for something . . . something to hold on to, something precious.

'Justin?' she whispered.

His body grew still and he drew back a little to look at her face. 'Yes?' His voice was oddly husky, and when he moved the hair away from his forehead, she noticed a slight tremble.

Feeling an infinite tenderness, she put her arms around him and drew him close again. 'Let's make love.' The words came softly, yet easily, reaching beyond the safe and secure, but she knew no doubt.

His arms tightened around her convulsively. 'I love you,' he said.

They went into the bedroom, taking only a candle, and in the shadowy light they took off their clothes. She felt a thrill of excitement at the sight of his naked body in front of her. He was looking at her too, his eyes taking in every part of her, but she felt no unease now, only a heady delight. He reached out to her. She moved towards him. Again they touched each other, sliding hands in gentle exploration along smooth skin and soft curves and hard muscles. Her body sang and every nerve ending quivered. There was a rush of powerful emotion, like falling water, rushing, rushing downward, unstoppable. She thought of the waterfalls, of standing naked in the sun, laughing, of the joy she had felt.

'You're smiling,' he whispered.

'You make me feel so good.'

His mouth quirked. 'I've only just got started.'

He kissed her deeply, his hands more urgent now, and her senses reeled. He was doing wonderful things to her body. The tension built till breaking point and desire was like an exquisite pain. Then suddenly there was no waiting any longer. A desperate urgency fired their lovemaking and swept them away to glorious, mutual fulfilment.

Her eyes closed, her heart beating at a frantic pace, she lay still in his arms. She could feel the rapid beating of his heart against her cheek. She wanted to lie there for ever, her face against his chest, their legs entwined, feeling the warmth of him, his strength and tenderness.

His hand was on her head, stroking her softly. 'Don't move,' he whispered.

In the morning she awoke finding him beside her, awake and watching her. A smile played around his mouth and she felt faint colour come to her cheeks. His smile broadened.

'Don't tell me you know how to blush.'

'How long have you been watching me?'

'A while.'

She knew from the way he looked at her that he wanted to make love again, but he made no attempt in that direction. 'Are you hungry?' he asked prosaically.

She shook her head. 'No.'

'I'll make us an omelette anyway. You need to eat before you go. You can't travel on an empty stomach.'

'I thought you might try and make me stay.'

He smiled crookedly. 'I'm tempted, believe me. But I think it would be a mistake. I think we need some time apart.' He jumped out of bed and wrapped a blue plaid sarong around his hips and left the bedroom.

Linden stared at the ceiling. He was right, of course. She should go home and nurse her fragile emotions back to health. Pelangi was supposed to have helped her recover from Waite. Now she was leaving to get herself straight about her feelings for another man. Fate certainly had no talent for timing.

Later, at the pier, she smiled a watery smile and he kissed her hard.

'See you in three months,' he said as he released her.

'Minus five days.' She turned and jumped into the boat. 'Please don't stand there and wave to me all the way across or I'll jump overboard and swim back.'

He grinned. 'Okay, okay, I'm going.' And with a wave of his arm he stalked back down the long rickety pier. She watched his retreating back, her throat thick with tears and suddenly paralysed by the fear that she was making a terrible mistake.

The trip home was endless. From Penang Airport she flew straight to Singapore without going back to mainland Malaysia. There were several hours to wait before her connecting flight and she wandered forlornly around the super modern Changi Airport looking uninterestedly at all the duty-free finery. At other times she might have been tempted by the perfumes, the designer jewellery or the Selangor pewter, but there were more important matters on her mind now, apart from the fact that she had no money to spend on luxuries.

She travelled without stopovers for sleep, and the hours and days blurred together as she dozed and slept and ate in one plane after another. In Los Angeles she called Liz to let her know her time of arrival in Philadelphia.

For two days, after she arrived, all she did was sleep and eat and then sleep some more. Then, in a sudden burst of new energy she packed up her belongings, arranged for storage, and packed her car for the trip south to New Orleans. She was eager to get out of town as fast as possible, before Waite could hear of her presence. The last thing she needed was to see him again.

The evening before Linden's departure Liz invited some of their friends for a small party and it was difficult then to realise what she was giving up. But there was no turning back now and she pushed the thought away.

Travelling by car in the dead of winter was not ideal, but at least she was going south and not north. In a way it was a peaceful trip across the country, all by herself, with only the car radio going. She ate at roadside restaurants and slept in motels, speaking to no one, meeting no one.

Stefanie was delighted to see her. Almost nine months pregnant she welcomed some help and companionship. She and her husband and their rapidly expanding family lived in a large sprawling old house with plenty of room to accommodate Linden for a while.

'You look so thin,' Stefanie remarked. 'Or is it because I'm so huge?'

'I'm thin and you're huge. Good Lord, are you manufacturing another set of twins?'

Stefanie laughed. 'The scan says no.'

Linden embraced her sister as best as she could, and

laughing they went inside where four small children descended on Linden for hugs and kisses.

The weeks that followed were anything but quiet. Stefanie gave birth to another baby boy. Linden ran the household as well as she could, cooking meals, tying bibs, wiping noses, bathing small, squealing, slippery bodies. Stefanie looked exhausted. Her husband Nick looked exhausted. Linden was exhausted. After her quiet life on Pelangi, this was bedlam. But four weeks later life for the family seemed to have returned to its normal state of happy disorder rather than the choas that had prevailed right after the birth. Linden had to admire Stefanie's stamina, her patience with her children, her obvious happiness with the new baby.

Linden managed to get out and explore New Orleans. She was offered help with this by one of Nick's colleagues, a young, divorced lawyer, who came for drinks one evening. He invited her out to dinner, which she refused politely, but firmly.

'What's the matter with you?' asked Stefanie after he had left.

'Nothing's the matter with me.'

'Why didn't you go out with him and have a good time?'

'I don't feel like it.'

'What's wrong with him?'

'I can't think of a thing, Stefanie. Young, good-looking, ambitious, good career, New England accent . . . Yale or Harvard?'

'Harvard. And he's even nice, Linden. I mean, he's *charming*. He has a sense of humour. Why couldn't you just go out with him? You don't have to *sleep* with the man. Although . . . I imagine that wouldn't be half-bad either.'

Linden sighed. 'I'm sure he's a real catch, Stefanie, but I'm simply not in the hunting mood.'

Stefanie shook her curly head in disapproval. 'How

long has it been since you broke up with Waite? Four months, five? Don't you think it's time to get yourself back in circulation?'

'Why?'

'Well . . . eh . . . it's *normal*! I mean, you're twenty-six years old. Don't you want a man in your life?'

'Are you worried I'm going to end up a sad, sour, shrivelled-up old spinster?'

Stefanie sighed. 'I just want you to be happy.'

'Well, I want to be happy too. And I hear the baby crying. You'd better feed the poor little critter.'

She managed to paint a little, but the children would not leave her alone, fascinated as they were by the paints and the brushes and the pictures. Her work was not up to par. Mostly she thought about Justin. He had finished his book and was back in New York. He'd sent her a cheque for the sale of the house and a short note. Even seeing the few words scrawled on the note had made her heart beat frantically. She saw his face everywhere, projected on the clouds, on store windows, on her bubble-bath soap-suds, on the page of a book she was reading. She carried his image with her all day—a mental photograph, a good luck charm. She wondered if he really loved her. *When I'm with you I feel . . . different, I feel good, as if life makes sense again.* His words echoed back into her mind. She wondered if she loved him.

What if she called his agent and he said sorry, Justin did not want to speak to her. What if she went to New York and realised it was all a mistake? They'd been alone on the island and drawn to each other naturally, but here, everything was different. Well, that's what these three months were for—to get everything back into perspective, to weed out the illusions and fantasies and see what was left. Maybe she should have gone out with the handsome Harvard man.

In three months all manner of things could have happened. She tried not to think of the various possibilities, but in unguarded moments her imagination ran wild.

Justin had decided he'd made a mistake.

He'd met another woman.

He'd met up again with Kate and she was getting a divorce.

He'd been in an accident and suffered from amnesia and did not recognise her.

He'd been in an accident and he was dead.

She began to have frightening dreams, waking up shaking and soaked with perspiration. She cursed herself for her neurotic fears.

She dreamed about making love to Justin again. It was an untenable situation. She wanted to be with him. She longed to see him and hear his voice and make love with him. Four more weeks to go. Three. Two.

She thought about Waite. There was regret and sadness where once had been pain. She wondered what had happened to him. She worried about it. It was a shock to see his handwriting on a letter addressed to her. Liz must have given him the address. She took the letter up to her room and slid it open with a fingernail, her heart in her throat. Damn, she thought, he can still do it to me.

The letter was short, only one page long, written by hand.

Dear Linden,

There are some things I need to say to you, so please bear with me and read this letter.

I want you to know what I will always love you, but I know that my love for you has not been a fair and giving love. Nothing has shaken me so much in my life as losing you. You loved me. I didn't think you would ever stop. I did not realise until later how difficult it must have been for you to stay with me as long as you did. I had no right to expect from you any more than you had already given me. Please forgive me the terrible things I said and did to you.

I'm seeing a counsellor. You urged me many times to find help, but I did not. I see now that, in some convoluted way, you saved me by leaving me. Had you not, I may never have admitted to having problems. When I came back from Pelangi, knowing I had lost you for good, that you could no longer stand by me, I had to face up to my problems.

I left Pelangi without saying goodbye. I didn't know how to do that. But maybe I am ready for that now too. So with this letter I am telling you goodbye. I wish you all the happiness you deserve. I will never forget you. My love, always, Waite.

Linden read and re-read the letter, going over the lines with tear-blurred eyes. The words were like a balm to the remnants of pain and regret still in the back of her mind. The dark weight of bitterness ebbed from her chest. Gently she put the paper down, feeling peace invade her. She wiped her eyes, 'Thank you, Waite,' she whispered. 'Thank you, thank you.'

Her finger was trembling as she pushed in the 'phone buttons.

'I would like to speak to Mr Cronin, please,' she said to the answering secretary. 'My name is Linden Mitchell.'

'Mr Cronin is in conference with a client. May I take a message?' A young voice, cool and impersonal.

Linden swallowed her disappointment. 'I want to contact Mr Parker. Justin Parker.'

There was a slight pause. 'You can leave a message for him if you like. Or write to him at this address.'

'I'd like to have his 'phone number, please.'

'I'm sorry, but I can't give out this information. It's against policies.'

'I see. I understand.' She tried not to have the irritation show in her voice. Of course it was only normal they didn't give out their clients' private addresses and 'phone numbers to anybody who asked for them. What was she to do now? 'I'd still like to speak to Mr Cronin then. Please give him my name and 'phone number and I'll wait for his call. Mr Parker should have mentioned my name to him.'

For the rest of the day she waited in vain for a call from New York. She was restless and irritable, and the children left her alone, sensing her state of mind.

'What's bothering you?' asked Stefanie, wiping apple sauce off the kitchen floor.

'I'm trying to contact somebody in New York and some battle-eager secretary is protecting him and I can't get a hold of him.'

'Well, you know about good secretaries. They have to protect their bosses from unwanted callers.'

'I'm not an unwanted caller, and if she's a good secretary she ought to know.'

'Secretaries are not all-seeing and all-knowing.'

'Then they shouldn't be secretaries.'

Stefanie rolled her eyes in exasperation as she rinsed out the cloth with which she'd been wiping the floor. 'Who are you trying to contact in New York?'

Linden hadn't told her sister anything about Justin, and Stefanie, Linden had to admit, had been good at not trying to pry too much for information.

'A man.' She took a tomato and cut it in pieces for the salad.

'That much I could guess.' Stefanie poured noodles in a pan of boiling water. On the back of the stove simmered a pan of minced-beef stroganoff. Nick would be home any minute now and the three grown-ups would have their dinner. He was home late every day and the children had already been fed and bathed and were happily playing for the moment.

'Actually, you know him, believe it or not.'

'I do? Who is it?'

'Justin Parker.'

Stefanie frowned and shrugged. 'Daddy had a friend named Parker. Leon or something. When he lived in Kuala Lumpur.'

'It's his son. He and his father came to Pelangi for Christmas dinner one year. I was sixteen.'

'Good heavens, that's ten years ago!' Stefanie bit the tip of her thumb in concentration, a habit she'd had since she'd been a child. 'I remember, vaguely.'

'It was that awful dinner with the tough chicken and the bad wine.'

Stefanie groaned. 'Yes, I remember now! Oh, Lord, that was so embarrassing!' She grinned. 'And how did you come across him again?'

'On Pelangi.' And then she told Stefanie the rest, leaving out the juicier details. But Stefanie, having a romantic mind, had no trouble imagining what Linden didn't tell. It was obvious in her eyes, but Linden said no more.

The next morning, Linden called again. The same girl answered the 'phone.

Linden took a mental breath. 'I haven't heard from either Mr Cronin or Mr Parker,' she stated bluntly.

'I'm sorry,' the girl said smoothly, 'but Mr Cronin had to leave immediately after his appointment yesterday and I'm afraid he didn't get a chance to return your call.'

Linden gritted her teeth. 'I'll right, we'll have to do something else then. I'm sorry to bother you with this, but it is important. It concerns the sale of Mr Parker's house in Malaysia and I need to speak to him urgently.' She was making it up, but she hoped this little bit of information about a house in some exotic part of the world would lend her plea some substance and credibility. 'I would appreciate it if you could contact him this very minute and give him my 'phone number and I'll be waiting to hear from him.'

There was a slight hesitation. 'I see. Well, I can try. I can't guarantee I'll get hold of him.'

'Keep trying until you get him, please.'

'I'll try.' It sounded reluctant.

'Thank you.' Linden replaced the receiver and looked at her watch.

Four minutes later the 'phone rang. She picked it up at the first ring, her heart suddenly racing in anticipation.

'Hello?'

'Miss Mitchell? The Cronin Agency. I called Justin Parker, but his answering service tells me he's gone to Connecticut and cannot be reached. He's expected back after the weekend.'

Linden felt her heart sink into her shoes. 'Did you leave a message?'

'Yes, I did.'

There was nothing to do but thank the girl and hang up. She felt utterly deflated. She stared at the pale blue telephone that matched the pale blue wall paper, bedspread and curtains of Stefanie's bedroom, and wondered what to do. Well, she wasn't going to sit around and wait any longer. It was time for some action. Now that she had made up her mind she was going, she might as well get started. She'd pack up the car and drive. It would take her a couple of days at least.

All through the long days on the road, doubts assailed her. What was Justin doing in Connecticut? Why couldn't he be reached? What if he had changed his mind and didn't want her anymore? And here she was with all her worldly goods in the car (except what was in storage), offering herself.

What if the meeting was a fiasco? After all, life on Pelangi was not life in New York. He would be different here. Undoubtedly she would be different here. Pelangi was months and many miles away—a dream, an illusion.

She'd never driven in New York and she got hopelessly lost, taking the wrong exits, going around the throughways in what seemed endless circles. When she finally made it into Manhattan, her hands were clammy and her clothes damp with perspiration. My God, what a jungle it was out here. She thought of Pelangi with its absence of cars, the peaceful paths, the empty beaches.

She found a parking space in an underground garage. By the end of the day she'd have to pay a fee that would feed her for an entire week on Pelangi.

The Cronin Agency had its offices in a building several blocks away and she walked in the April sunshine, glad for the exercise after sitting for so long. It was Monday. Maybe Justin was back in town today. Maybe in an hour or so she'd be with him. She hurried into the building giving her name to the balding doorman and stating her business. She found a ladies' room to make repairs to her appearance. She combed her hair, washed her hands, applied fresh make-up. Her heart was beating nervously. With a deep breath for courage she walked determinedly down the long, carpeted floor to the Cronin Literary Agency.

A girl with short honey-blonde hair and green eyes sat behind the reception desk, typing. She was beautiful, dressed in a skirt and well-fitting silk blouse. She gave Linden a cool look.

'I'm Linden Mitchell,' she announced herself.

'I know. The doorman called me.' She did not shut off the typewriter. 'Mr Cronin is not in and Mr Parker has not yet returned from Connecticut.' There was speculation in her eyes as she observed Linden, taking in her jeans and shirt and sweater-jacket.

'When was the last time you called?'

'Two minutes ago, right before you came up. I'm sorry, but there is nothing I can do for you.'

She didn't seem sorry in the least. She's probably in

love with him, Linden thought. The new and up-coming writer of spy novels—handsome, virile and with a tropical tan in early April.

'All right, thank you, I'll be back in the morning.'

She rode down in the elevator, angry and disappointed. Justin Parker, where are you when I want you?

She asked the doorman for the address of a hotel nearby, something not too fancy or expensive. He told her where to go, giving directions, chatting. Was she new in New York? He thought so. He could always tell. Where was she from? He had a slight Irish lilt and a friendly grin, not at all what you expected of New Yorkers, who were supposed to be dour, unsmiling and too wrapped up in themselves to give anyone the time of day.

The hotel was small and old, but clean. After she'd settled in, she went out again, explored Manhattan on foot, and for dinner had a generous plate of Linguini Alfredo in a small Italian restaurant complete with Italian-speaking waiters.

At nine the next morning, after a restless night, she rode the elevator back up to the Cronin Agency's offices. She didn't care what the girl thought of her. All she cared about now was seeing Justin, even if she had to sit in the office all day and wait.

When she opened the door it wasn't the girl she saw, but Justin's back. He was leaning against the desk, talking to the girl, stopping in mid-sentence when he turned and saw Linden enter.

Her heart pounded like a sledgehammer. A short, trimmed beard covered the lower part of his face. He wore tailored slacks instead of shorts or a sarong, a teal blue sweater, sleeves pushed up to the elbows, a tweed jacket slung over his shoulder. His appearance was a shock. She'd known he would look different, somehow, but not this different, not like a bearded stranger.

'Excuse me,' he said to the girl in the sudden quiet that had fallen over the reception room. He took Linden's arm and propelled her out of the door into the deserted hallway.

They faced each other. There was a smile in his eyes. 'Well, this is a surprise.'

She swallowed, feeling awkward and uncertain. 'I hope you don't mind I came a little earlier than planned. I tried to call, but I couldn't get through.'

'I was in Connecticut. I only came back last night. I called my telephone service and they told me you were in town but they didn't know where. They said you'd be here in the morning, so here I am too.' His smile deepened. 'You look nervous.'

'Me? Nervous?' she asked brightly. 'However did you get that idea? You look strange.'

'So do you, with that jacket on. I tend to picture you wearing a sarong.' He leaned against the wall, observing her with humour in his eyes.

'I still wear a sarong around the house.'

'Good. I like that.'

'How's everything with your book? Did the movie-deal come through?' she asked, rubbing her clammy hands on the side of her jeans. She didn't know why she felt so funny all of a sudden. Why this man who looked like Justin and sounded like Justin, seemed a stranger.

He straightened away from the wall. 'They're still working on the details. I'll tell you all about it over a cup of coffee at my place.' He took her arm again and led her down the hall to the bank of elevators.

'How did you get here?' he asked as they left the building.

'I drove.' The sunshine made her blink. A cool breeze stroked her face.

'Very brave. Where did you park the car?'

'In a garage three blocks down that way.' She pointed left.

'All right, let's get it. What about your luggage? Where did you stay last night?'

She pointed in the opposite direction. 'Two blocks thataway, turn right, middle of the block.'

They got the car. 'You drive,' she suggested, handing him the keys. 'You know where we're going.' He grinned and took the keys without comment. They picked up her things at the hotel and drove on to Justin's apartment.

'This place is intimidating,' she said. 'I drove around for an hour yesterday getting lost all over the place. I felt really stupid.'

'It does take some getting used to.'

'You like New York?'

'In small doses, yes. There's a lot to see and do and it's a dynamic place. But I did get addicted to my peace and quiet on Pelangi.'

The apartment was sumptuous. Thick carpeting, white upholstered Swedish furniture, modern art on the wall, a bar.

'I'm impressed,' she said, looking around in awe.

He grinned. 'Unfortunately it's not mine. I'm subletting it for a couple of months. I was lucky to get it. It belongs to one of Cronin's friends who's spending the winter months in warmer climes.' He'd dropped her things in the hallway and was reaching for her jacket. She loosened the leather belt and slid it off her shoulders. He hung it in the hall closet and she followed him to the kitchen. He filled the electric coffee maker with water and ground coffee.

'So, how did you fare these last few months?' The question was asked casually.

She lowered herself on a kitchen stool. 'I went back to Pennsylvania, packed up my stuff, put most of it in storage and drove my poor little Chevy to New Orleans, where my sister Stefanie awaited me with a huge belly and open arms.'

'How did you get along this time?'

'Better. I think she was afraid I'd walk out and leave her, and she needed me. The baby was born two weeks after I arrived, another boy. The house was in chaos. Five kids under five, you can imagine.'

He shook his head. 'No, I can't. It's beyond me.' He gave a boyish grin. 'You seem to have survived it.'

'Appearances are deceptive.'

He laughed. 'What did she think about you staying with her for such a long time?'

'I told her I was finished with Waite and I needed a change of scene.'

There was a slight pause. 'Did you see him while you were packing up your apartment?'

She looked at him. 'No. I don't know if he knew I was there or not. I didn't go anywhere. I was in and out of town in a matter of days.'

She thought of the letter Waite had written her. For a fleeting moment she considered showing it to Justin, then rejected the idea. It had been a letter to her only. What had happened between them was private. He had said goodbye to her and it was over now.

The coffee pot was making gurgling noises and a rich aroma filled the kitchen.

'Have you had breakfast yet?' he asked.

'No.'

'I didn't think so.' He shook his head in disapproval. 'Breakfast is the most important meal of the day. Don't you read the papers?'

'Shut up, Justin. I don't want to hear about it.'

He laughed out loud. 'Now you sound like the Linden I know.'

She smiled back at him, lightheaded. His eyes held hers for a long moment, then he reached for her hands. Her pulse began to race.

'What are you going to say when I kiss you?' he asked. ' "No, Justin!" "Stop it, Justin!" "I warn you, Justin!" '

'Why don't you try and find out?' she said lightly. 'I might come up with something more creative.' *Hold me. Kiss me!*

'Mmm ... am I going to like it?'

'I don't know. You'll have to take your chances. I'm a creature of whims and sudden urges. You never know what I'll come up with.'

He threw back his head and laughed. 'You've got yourself all wrong, sweetheart.'

'You think you know me so well,' she taunted.

'I do that. But I must admit the process hasn't been easy.' His eyes narrowed slightly. 'Why did you come two weeks early?'

'You know me so well, you tell me.'

'You couldn't stand those screaming kids anymore.'

'Actually they're very good. Stefanie really knows how to handle them. I might change my mind and have five myself.'

He groaned. 'You're changing the subject.'

'I am? What were we talking about?'

'Why you came two weeks early.'

'Oh, well, let's see. Actually, I was worried about you.'

'*Worried?*'

'I was wondering what the big city might do to you after three years on Pelangi. All those sophisticated girls, like the green-eyed blonde at the reception desk at the agency. I thought I'd better check to see if you needed any protection.'

There was a gleam of laughter in his eyes. *He looks wonderful*, she thought. *I like that beard—it looks sexy. I've never kissed a man with a beard.*

He drew her slowly to him, looking into her eyes, and she put her arms around his neck, her heart throbbing wildly. She stood very still as he lowered his face. The beard touched her skin and it sent a thrill of excitement through her. His lips moved over hers, softly, tantalising. 'I missed you,' he whispered against her lips.

She felt the glow of euphoria, a singing. 'I missed you too.'

CHAPTER NINE

HE moulded her body against his and his smouldering, kiss sent heat waves through her body. *I'm going to melt at his feet. How embarrassing.* Breathlessly, she moved her face and put it against his shoulder.

It took a few moments to catch her breath. 'I've never kissed a man with a beard,' she said against his neck. 'It's doing terrifying things to my heart.'

'I'll shave it off, if you want,' he whispered.

'Oh, no! I like it! It's a very sexy beard. Why did you grow it?'

'It was so damn cold when I came here. Why are you laughing?'

She raised her head to look at him. 'I once had an English friend who told me men grow beards to cover up weak chins.'

His lips curled in amusement. 'I guess I'm in trouble then. Everybody is going to think I have a weak chin. I'm a weak person. The dregs of society.'

The word weak would not enter anybody's head looking at this man. She didn't want him to shave the beard, ever. She raised her arm and ran her fingers over the short dark hair. 'I wouldn't worry about it if I were you. A lot of women think beards are sexy.'

He let out a deep sigh. 'That's a big relief.'

Why are we standing here talking? The tension was mounting. She could feel the heat of his body against her. She was taken over by an overwhelming physical feeling and breathing was difficult.

'What about the coffee?' she asked.

He gave her a long look. 'You want coffee?'

She nodded. 'Yes.'

'No, you don't.' His hands slid down her thighs and

drew her close against him.

'Justin . . .'

He led her into the bedroom. She felt weak as water, her head light. The room was bright with spring sunshine and he moved to the windows and drew the curtains across. In the muted, filtered light she saw him come towards her and she moved into his arms. He began to kiss her, his hands moving slowly but surely, taking off her clothes.

They were on the big bed, naked in the pale light. His hands gently circled her breasts and her body sang to his touch. She looked at him as he leaned over her, touching his chest, his stomach. The feel of the clean lines of his body excited her.

'Oh, God, Linden,' he whispered and the urgency in his voice made her senses quiver. His mouth closed over her breast, kissing her softly, then slowly moved down. He did the most wonderful things to her body, setting it ablaze with exquisite sensation. The ecstasy was almost unbearable and finally the excitement was too much and he groaned and drew her fiercely to him. Everything faded into oblivion and there was only her awareness of him and the love that carried them to ecstasy.

For a while afterwards they did not speak, but lay silently in each other's arms, relishing the sweet contentment of the moment.

They were hungry then, and he brought a tray of food to the bedroom. They ate, hungry as mountain climbers, sitting up in bed—Swedish crisp bread and French goat cheese, an apple, coffee and chocolate cake.

'This is the weirdest breakfast I've ever had,' she said. 'Delicious, though.'

'It's eleven-thirty. It's brunch.'

She smiled sunnily. 'Whatever you say.'

'Let's go to Connecticut.'

'Connecticut? Why?'

'I bought a house. I want you to see it.'

She couldn't wait.

They drove down the New York Turnpike, slowing down near Greenwich to go through the toll gates, on to the Connecticut turnpike. The sun shone on the still-bare trees, but green was visible here and there, and the bright colour of crocus and daffodils in well-tended beds. They took the Westport exit and drove along long winding roads. Large, beautiful old houses lay back from the roads, surrounded by maples and oaks and evergreens.

'It's beautiful here,' said Linden. 'Those houses . . . it looks like an affluent community. Quite a difference from my little town in Pennsylvania.'

'Don't you like rich people?' There was a smile in his voice.

'I'm not used to rich people.'

'Well, not everybody is rich here. There are many ordinary middle-class American citizens in Westport.'

'Tell me about it, about the town. What kind of place is it?'

'Well, let's see. There's quite an artist colony here—writers, painters, sculptors, actors, the lot. And not all of them are famous either, so don't let that intimidate you. There are art galleries and art supply stores and craft shops and places like that. It's a New England town—white clapboard houses, small churches, small-town shops—antique stores and health food stores and spice shops along with the hardware store and the dry cleaners. But it has a character all its own. It's not as sleepy as some of the towns further north. There are a number of restaurants and coffee bars with jazz bands and live piano music and there is an amateur theatre group. In many ways it's very small-townish, but the people are quite sophisticated. New York, of course, is right down the road, and many people commute to work, and go there for plays and concerts.'

'It sounds interesting.'

'I hope you'll like it here.'

I hope you'll like it here. 'You want me to move to Westport with you?' she asked.

He gave her a quick sideways glance. 'I was hoping you would.'

She wondered what he had in mind. Did he expect her to move in with him? Did he want to marry her? They'd have to talk about it. She'd better figure out what it was she wanted herself. Decisions to change the course of her life. She had no job now and didn't know if she could find work in a place like this. Anxiety curled in her stomach and her throat was dry.

'There's a big party a couple of weeks from now,' Justin was saying. 'I got an invitation just yesterday. I'm sure it won't be difficult to meet people we like.'

'No, I suppose not.' *Maybe all he wants is an affair. Why haven't I thought about this before? Why do I always think in terms of forever? That's one of the reasons I was so devastated about leaving Waite.*

Fear crept over her. Oh, for heaven's sake, she said to herself, calm down. You don't have to decide anything today. Or even next week. Just enjoy being with him. Right now that's all that matters. It will all work itself out. She shifted in her seat, trying to relax, gazing at the scenery outside.

They said nothing more until he took a left and slowed down.

'Is your house here?'

'The next one on the right.'

The house was several hundred feet from the road and the drive was long and narrow, flanked by pines. When the house came into view she looked at it with delight—dark wood, white-painted window frames, a big stone chimney covered with ivy. A house out of a picture.

He opened the door and she climbed out of the car.

He smiled down at her. 'What do you think?'

'It's beautiful.'

'Wait till everything is green. I saw colour photos. Look at those azaleas over there. It'll be quite a scene when they're all in bloom.' He took a key from his pocket and opened the heavy front door. 'Welcome home,' he said, waving her in with an expansive gesture. They entered a small hall with an open archway leading into a large living room empty of furniture.

Linden walked through the rooms in a daze. It was a house with character and warmth and atmosphere, even without furniture. It was at least a hundred years old and maintained meticulously. There were gleaming oak floors, a field stone fire place in the living room, and a flagstone terrace overlooking the Naugatuck river. Woods stretched out beyond the river and the house was surrounded by large pines and firs. The kitchen was done in natural-stained oak and the modern appliances were all craftily hidden behind oak panelling. There were several bedrooms with luxuriously soft carpeting, all empty.

'I ordered a bed and mattress,' said Justin. 'It should be delivered tomorrow.'

'Where will we stay tonight?'

He rested his arms lightly on her shoulders and smiled into her eyes. 'Well, as I see it, we have two choices. One: We can check into a motel. Two: We can go to the sports shop and buy a couple of sleeping bags. We can zip them together and camp out on the floor in here.' He moved his foot over the carpeting. 'This looks nice and thick. Should be all right for one night.' He looked at her expectantly. 'What do you think?'

She stood on tip toe and put her mouth against his. 'Going to a motel is so tacky,' she whispered against his lips. 'I want to stay here.'

'I hoped you'd say that.' He kissed her, then drew

away, laughing lights in his eyes. 'You haven't seen everything yet.'

She clung to him. 'I don't care.' She felt wanton, light-headed. She wanted to make love. Now. Here. On the floor.

'Oh, but you will.' He took her hand and led her through another door. 'How do you like this?'

It was a study lined with empty bookshelves. Near the window stood a large battered wooden desk on top of which sat, incongruously, a sleek, shiny computer unit with a small television-type screen.

Linden gave a soft laugh. 'You weren't kidding, were you? About a computer?'

'A word processor. This one is specifically pro-grammed for that. See, this is the printer. Marvellous machine. I'll teach you how it works.'

'No thanks. Fancy machines like that are not for me.'

He was grinning at her. 'All you need is a few manual paint brushes and some pots of paint, right?'

'You've got it.'

Justin reached for a door in one of the walls. 'See this door? Was just put in a couple of days ago.'

'There's *another* room?'

He nodded. 'It has its entrance off the hall. You probably didn't see it. It's built a little funny, this house. I thought it would be more practical to have a door between these two rooms.' He swung the door open, went in ahead of her and turned to face her. 'For you,' he said, watching her.

The bright light made her blink a few times. Another empty room. White walls. Sunlight streaming in through two large glass sliding doors with a view of the river. On the other side the room had a slanting roof with a large skylight built into it.

She couldn't believe her eyes. An indescribable feeling of elation filled her. 'A studio,' she whispered. 'A real studio!' Her eyes filled with tears. 'You were thinking of me when you bought this house, weren't you?'

He smiled crookedly. 'That's why I bought it. Because it had this room. There were other houses, some nicer than this one, but none had a room like this.'

'Oh, Justin! I don't know what to say!' She was laughing while tears rolled down her face. She threw her arms around him and pressed her face against his shoulder. 'It's the nicest present I've ever had.'

'I thought that was the cheddar I got you from Penang.'

'You just managed to top it.' She kissed him fiercely. 'You're wonderful you know. And to think I nearly let you go!'

'*I* wasn't about to let *you* go, though.'

'I'm sorry I was so awful.'

'I'll forgive you.'

She sighed. 'I'm glad. Justin?'

'What?'

'There's something I haven't told you yet.'

'What?'

She looked into his eyes and swallowed hard. 'I love you. I love you very much.'

His arms tightened around her and he put his face against hers. 'I love you too, Linden,' he said huskily.

For a while they stood silently in each other's arms.

'What are we going to do about us?' he asked at last. 'Do you want to live together for ever and ever, or get married?'

She gave a low laugh. 'We can do both.'

He grinned. 'You're absolutely right.'

'It might be better for the children.'

'True. How many?'

She smiled brightly. 'Oh, five at least.'

Here's how to get this special offer from Harlequin!
As simple as 1...2...3!

OCTOBER
TREASURY EDITION
COUPON

1. Each month, save one Treasury Edition coupon from your favorite Romance or Presents novel.
2. In four months you'll have saved four Treasury Edition coupons (<u>only one coupon per month allowed</u>).
3. Then all you have to do is fill out and return the order form provided, along with the four Treasury Edition coupons required and $1.00 for postage and handling.

Mail to: Harlequin Reader Service

In the U.S.A.
2504 West Southern Ave.
Tempe, AZ 85282

In Canada
P.O. Box 2800, Postal Station A
5170 Yonge Street
Willowdale, Ont. M2N 6J3

RT1-C-2

Please send me my FREE copy of the Janet Dailey Treasury Edition. I have enclosed the four Treasury Edition coupons required and $1.00 for postage and handling along with this order form.

(Please Print)

NAME_____

ADDRESS_____

CITY_____

STATE/PROV._____ ZIP/POSTAL CODE_____

SIGNATURE_____

This offer is limited to one order per household.

SUPPLIES LIMITED

This special Janet Dailey offer expires January 1986.

H·A·R·L·E·Q·U·I·N

FIRST·CLASS
Sweepstakes

OFFICIAL RULES

1. NO PURCHASE NECESSARY. To enter, complete the official entry/order form. Be sure to indicate whether or not you wish to take advantage of our subscription offer.

2. Entry blanks have been preselected for the prizes offered. Your response will be checked to see if you are a winner. In the event that these preselected responses are not claimed, a random drawing will be held from all entries received to award not less than $150,000 in prizes. This is in addition to any free, surprise or mystery gifts which might be offered. Versions of this sweepstakes with different prizes will appear in Preview Service Mailings by Harlequin Books and their affiliates. Winners selected will receive the prize offered in their sweepstakes brochure.

3. This promotion is being conducted under the supervision of Marden-Kane, an independent judging organization. By entering the sweepstakes, each entrant accepts and agrees to be bound by these rules and the decisions of the judges, which shall be final and binding. Odds of winning in the random drawing are dependent upon the total number of entries received. Taxes, if any, are the sole responsibility of the prize winners. Prizes are nontransferable. All entries must be received by August 31, 1986.

4. The following prizes will be awarded:

   (1) Grand Prize: Rolls-Royce™ *or* $100,000 Cash!
   (Rolls-Royce being offered by permission of Rolls-Royce Motors Inc.)

   (1) Second Prize: A trip for two to Paris for 7 days/6 nights. Trip includes air transportation on the Concorde, hotel accommodations...PLUS...$5,000 spending money!

   (1) Third Prize: A luxurious Mink Coat!

5. This offer is open to residents of the U.S. and Canada, 18 years or older, except employees of Harlequin Books, its affiliates, subsidiaries, Marden-Kane and all other agencies and persons connected with conducting this sweepstakes. All Federal, State and local laws apply. Void in the province of Quebec and wherever prohibited or restricted by law. Winners will be notified by mail and may be required to execute an affidavit of eligibility and release, which must be returned within 14 days after notification. Canadian winners will be required to answer a skill-testing question. Winners consent to the use of their name, photograph and/or likeness for advertising and publicity purposes in conjunction with this and similar promotions without additional compensation. One prize per family or household.

6. For a list of our most current prize winners, send a stamped, self-addressed envelope to: WINNERS LIST, c/o Marden-Kane, P.O. Box 10404, Long Island City, New York 11101

You're invited to accept 4 books and a surprise gift Free!

Acceptance Card

Mail to: Harlequin Reader Service®

In the U.S.
2504 West Southern Ave.
Tempe, AZ 85282

In Canada
P.O. Box 2800, Postal Station A
5170 Yonge Street
Willowdale, Ontario M2N 6J3

YES! Please send me 4 free Harlequin Presents® novels and my free surprise gift. Then send me 8 brand new novels every month as they come off the presses. Bill me at the low price of $1.75 each ($1.95 in Canada)—an 11% saving off the retail price. There are no shipping, handling or other hidden costs. There is no minimum number of books I must purchase. I can always return a shipment and cancel at any time. Even if I never buy another book from Harlequin, the 4 free novels and the surprise gift are mine to keep forever.

108 BPP-BPGE

Name _____ (PLEASE PRINT)

Address _____ Apt. No. _____

City _____ State/Prov. _____ Zip/Postal Code _____

This offer is limited to one order per household and not valid to present subscribers. Price is subject to change.

ACP-SUB-1